Fated Bloodlines

G Clatworthy

Foreword

This story takes place in the Rise of Dragons universe; a world where magical and mundane beings coexist and dragons have recently been awoken.

The first three books in the Rise of Dragons series are told from the point of view of Amethyst Haernson, a half-dwarf jeweller who just wants a quiet life. Book 4 shows Special Agent Ruth Jones' point of view and is set in parallel to the end of Book 2 and part of Book 3. In Book 5 and this book, we're back to Amethyst's point of view. Now we're all caught up, read on…

If you want to support Gemma, you can find her on patreon.com/G_Clatworthy for exclusive first reads of new stories. You can also join her newsletter for a free prequel to this series and follow Gemma on www.instagram.com/gemmaclatworthy, www.facebook.com/gemmaclatworthy or join the reader's group Gemma's book wyrms.

Chapter 1

I caught the elf looking at me askance. Out of the corner of his bright green eyes.

"Are you alright?"

"What? Yes, fine," Lorandir's voice was higher than usual, as if he was nervous. I pursed my lips together. He had seemed jumpy back in the Dragon's Head café when we had ordered some of the luscious chocolate brownies and a couple of coffees to go from the owner, Brinda. At the time, I thought he was just annoyed that we had forgotten our reusable mugs and had bought new ones. I thought they were sweet with the Dragon's Head logo printed neatly on bamboo but maybe it brought back too many memories of dragon attacks for my boyfriend.

He stepped out into the road.

"What are you doing?!" I pulled on his arm, yanking him back onto the pavement.

Lorandir shook his head, "Sorry, I thought it was green." He pushed a hand through his blonde hair distractedly. What was going on with him today?

There were a lot of tourists out in Cardiff today and most of them seemed to be at the same pedestrian crossing as we waited for the traffic lights to turn green so we could cross safely. I pulled Errol's lead tightly as the small wyrm tried to snap at the ankles of someone in front of us. The last thing I needed was the dragon-like creature harming someone. I could imagine exactly what my Uncle Owain, owner of a wyrm farm in the Welsh countryside, would say. It wouldn't make pleasant listening.

A black taxi zoomed through the red light, nearly taking out a group of Chinese tourists heading to Cardiff Castle. I wasn't sure of the exact words one of the tourists used as he shook his fist after the cab driver, but the message was clear. Good on him. His friends hurried him over the crossing. I watched them turn onto the wooden drawbridge that led to the enormous gate in the castle walls.

This week was the first time the castle had been opened to the public since a dragon slumbering under its foundations had awakened last year, causing half the castle to collapse. I remembered it well. I had been there as the creature had fought its way to the surface. The castle itself was still closed for repairs but the grounds and the domineering stone keep were back open for business. A member of the royal family had even been here to re-open it. I had seen it on the news. There had been a ribbon and everything.

Lorandir's shoulders relaxed as the crowd formed a large queue in front of the gate and we carried on to Bute Park. Maybe he was just feeling claustrophobic. There were a lot of people out today enjoying the sunshine on the hot summer's day. I instinctively swapped sides with the elf, so I was nearest to the road as we walked along the pavement next to the stone wall that linked Cardiff Castle to Bute Park. The stonemason had decided to top the wall with lifelike carved animals crawling over the top and had completed the look with realistic, menacing glass eyes. I didn't like any of them, but the baboon was the worst. It always seemed like it was about to jump down and go on a rampage.

Normally Lorandir would argue good-naturedly that the man should be nearest the traffic. Today…he was silent. Schiztz. An unwelcome thought formed in my head. Was he going to break up with me? I studied his attractive face again. He looked distracted and kept giving me those sideways glances.

He started smiling slightly as we approached the park's iron gates. I could put it down to his love of nature. Being an elf, he was always more comfortable around trees…or was it relief that he'd soon be finished with me? I thought back over our time together.

"How's your training going with Espretha?" he asked.

Schiztz. Now he was bringing up his gorgeous elf friend. Our relationship had been going well. At least, I thought it had. Not that I had much in the way of relationships to compare it to. We'd spent almost every night together, especially since we'd almost been killed in Avalon last year. I'd been enjoying our relationship, but maybe it had been too much for him.

Aware my thoughts were spiralling instead of answering his question, I pulled myself back to the conversation, "Yeah, good, I guess."

A honking horn and a squeal of tyres pulled me out of my self-pitying introspection. I turned to the road in time to see a flash of something blue cross the tarmac.

The cars weren't exactly going fast thanks to the usual heavy weekend traffic and the constant pedestrians using the crossing, but it was tricky to stop. A yellow mini's wheel clipped the small blue creature and sent it careening into the kerb. I heard a yelp of pain and saw the small pictsie trying to scrabble off the road. More cars drove past, ignoring the small creature's plight. I walked towards it. Its black eyes met mine and it froze in shock, curling in on itself in a small ball. I had to do something.

I held my hands out and stepped into the road, blocking the cars while I rescued the fallen pictsie. More horns honked as I blocked the inner lane of traffic from moving. I moved Errol's lead from hand to hand as I felt in my jean pockets for something to wrap around the shocked fae creature. Nothing.

I briefly considered tearing a strip from my top. No good. I was wearing a corset top with boning built in. I liked the steampunk style, and it suited my curvy figure, but it wasn't good for makeshift rescuing material.

"What are you playing at love?" a driver shouted from a convertible.

Lorandir joined me in the road and took Errol off me. "So, what's the plan?" He seemed amused.

"Give me your top."

"Pardon?"

"I need something to pick up the pictsie with. Take off your top."

With a sigh, the elf complied and pulled off his forest green t-shirt, revealing his toned torso. He threw it over to me and folded his arms self-consciously as he stared down two women who wolf-whistled at him from across the road. I turned to the creature and whispered words of comfort as I scooped it up in the fabric.

"There now, you'll be OK. We'll just take you to the park and check you're alright," I crooned to the creature. I stepped back onto the pavement and motioned to Lorandir to follow me. Errol gave a small growl as he scented the fae creature in my arms. Once we were safely through the iron gates, I cautiously opened the folded t-shirt to see if the small pictsie had been hurt.

The creature was as big as my hand and the same dark blueish-purple colour as a ripe blueberry. Large, black eyes blinked up at me and it partially uncurled itself from the protective ball shape it had formed. It was vaguely humanoid with feet and hands that ended with sharp pointed claws. I looked it up and down. I couldn't see anything wrong with it but I wasn't a vet.

"We need to call someone, take it to a rescue centre or something."

Lorandir had his phone out and shook his head, "We can't do that. Outside of Cornwall, these things are classed as pests. If we take it in, they'll have to put it down."

I gasped as the elf showed me his phone screen, confirming what he'd said. I looked down at the helpless creature laying still in my hands. It looked up at me with its large, dark eyes.

"I can't keep you, sorry, you'll have to make it here by yourself." It stared up at me reproachfully. I didn't know if it could understand me, but it was doing a good job of making me feel guilty. I put it down on the grass. "Go on, go!"

I waved my hand over it in a shooing motion to get it to go away. It stood and gripped my index finger in its tiny hands. I sniffed slightly, suddenly emotional. The pictsie was saying thank you to me. It was so sweet, in a bug-like sort of way. I smiled down at it. I felt a strange sensation behind me; that sharp feeling you get when someone is staring at you. I thought I caught an impression of blood and fire. It reminded me of the evil magic I'd witnessed in Avalon last year.

I turned my attention back to the pictsie which had tightened its grip on my hand, its claws digging gently into my skin. It opened its mouth in a smile, revealing a full set of pointed teeth. I smiled back. It bit down hard on my finger.

"Ow! Sonofa…!" I shook my hand out to dislodge the creature. It clamped on hard, and blood trickled down my palm. I shook harder and flung it off towards a tree. It turned a somersault in mid-air and suddenly it had wings. The dzraker flew away. It turned back and chattered at me before flying up into the nearest tree. I heard a thump and hoped it had hit its head on a branch. Hard.

I shook my hand again and surveyed the damage. Blood oozed from the wound. Dzraking pictsies. No wonder they were called pests. Lorandir took my hand in his and studied it carefully. I felt his familiar intoxicating magic fill me. Somehow it reminded me of honey mead, bittersweet dark chocolate and leafy forests all in one. It was intense. The pain in my finger subsided as his healing magic coursed through me and closed the wound. I wiped the blood left on my hand on my jeans. I hoped it would come out in the wash. Most of my trousers already had small burn marks from crafting jewellery and this was a nice pair of jeans; dark enough that I could get away with wearing them out in the evening as well as during the day.

"We should take you to a hospital," Lorandir interrupted my thoughts. He was staring at my finger.

"It's fine, you healed it. Now where are those brownies? I need some sugar after that blood loss."

The elf arched an eyebrow at me, "That article said pictsie bites can be poisonous and I'm not sure my magic works on that."

"Don't even worry about it," I said around a mouthful of heavenly chocolate brownies. Lorandir frowned, clearly unhappy with my devil may care attitude to my health. To his credit, he merely put on his t-shirt, now stained with my blood and a strange blue smear that I didn't want to think too hard about, and offered me his arm. We strolled through the park. The leafy trees provided pleasant shade on the hot day, and we picked a large oak to sit under and finish our coffees and brownies. I let Errol off his lead and laughed as he used his small wings to jump and glide along, chasing after bugs.

"Amethyst, I love your laugh," the elf traced one long finger along the side of my face before pulling back. "I hope you know I've enjoyed our time together," he continued. Schiztz. I'd forgotten he was about to break up with me. My face froze in a strange half smile. "It's been the best time of my life actually; I've never felt more alive and…" he let out a grunt of frustration and raked a hand through his blonde hair. He'd kept it shorter than the usual elven hairstyles and, when he tussled it, it looked like he should be part of a boy band. I'd miss the feel of that silken hair against my fingers. I reached out, desperate for one last brush before he ended it.

"Er…" I tried to interrupt.

"Please, Ame, Amethyst, let me finish. What I'm trying to say is…" he pulled both of my hands into his own. I felt the contrast of his soft skin with my own calloused hands. No matter how much hand cream I used, it never made up for my days spent at the forge where I crafted my jewellery and weapons. He looked down, "…your finger is turning blue!"

Chapter 2

"Don't even worry…" I started to say. I trailed off as I looked down at my finger. It had swollen to twice its normal size and was indeed a shade of blue. It was the sort of blueish grey that you might find on a recently deceased zombie in a horror film. Schiztz. I prodded it with my other hand and winced. It was painful to the touch, like a spark set off under my skin. Lorandir's magic furled into me again. I waited. My finger stayed the colour of an undead marshmallow and the pain, when I touched it, was still there.

"Let's get you to a hospital."

I shook my head, "Let's give it another hour. I'll go if it gets any worse."

"We're going to the hospital now!"

Lorandir dragged me to my feet, carefully avoiding my poisoned finger, and marched me out of the park. Errol darted around my feet, nearly causing me to trip up twice. After the second time, I picked him up, carefully avoiding my swollen finger. The small wyrm struggled in my arms. I knew how he felt. It was hot. Too hot to be carrying a creature that always

15

felt like a small furnace. I wiped away a bead of sweat; my hair stuck to my face in clumpy strands.

With a final twist and a dig of his claws, Errol jumped up onto Lorandir's shoulders and curled around his neck happily. I mumbled something about ungrateful pets as I rubbed the scratches on my arm. They stung more than my blue finger, and I cursed softly.

Once back at the main road, Lorandir stepped to the edge of the pavement and lifted his arm in the universal signal for needing a taxi. One came to a halt almost immediately. Typical. The elf ushered me inside and told the driver to get us to the hospital fast. The driver eyed the small dragon-like creature around my boyfriend's neck and instantly added a tenner to the fare.

"If he causes any damage, you will have to pay!"

Lorandir nodded and stroked Errol calmly. The wyrm opened one amber eye and a tendril of smoke curled up from one nostril. I closed my eyes, willing him not to burn anything.

The taxi driver must have wanted us out of his cab as fast as possible. He swerved through the busy weekend traffic in record time, dodging into non-existent gaps and weaving his way to the front of every queue. I heard some terse curse words in a foreign language as he cut up another taxi and got into the fastest moving lane. Lorandir spent the drive soothing Errol, who growled softly at every erratic motion of the vehicle and resting his cool hand on my feverish forehead. It was unfair that in this sweltering weather, he was unaffected.

Eventually, the taxi pulled up to the University Hospital of Wales. I stared out of the window at the mural painted on the side. It showed a red Welsh dragon on a blue background. The dragon had its mouth open and looked like it was puking bright yellow daffodils. I frowned and wondered what the artist was trying to convey.

I tried to take a picture for my Uncle Owain; he owned a wyrm farm in the Welsh countryside and had strong views about artists romanticising dragons. I prodded the screen with my uninjured hand as we sped past. The photo came out as blurs of red and yellow on my phone.

The taxi screeched to a halt outside the walk-in accident and emergency unit. It was a tall, grey building, fashioned, like so many public buildings, from grim concrete on the outskirts of the city. Lorandir paid the fare and then practically pushed me through the automatic sliding doors to the check-in desk. A tired-looking receptionist in a crisp white shirt looked up at us. She slid a form attached to a cheap clipboard across the counter, followed by a chewed biro. I tried to pick it up and winced at the pressure of the pen on my index finger.

The receptionist motioned for us to move so she could check in the newest patient who had walked through the door; a child in a football kit limping next to a harried mother. Obediently, we moved to some uncomfortable wooden chairs, and I switched to my other hand and tried to fill out the form. I wrote my name in a child-like scrawl of badly formed capital letters before Lorandir took the pen from me. He fired questions at me as he completed the form with flowing cursive penmanship. We both hesitated over the tick box for magical beings or human. I was half and half. I pointed to the human box. Maybe I'd get seen more quickly if the hospital thought I was fully human. He paused again at the large box for the type of injury.

"Just write that a dzraking pictsie bit my finger and now it's dzraking blue!" I lost my patience. With a half-smile, Lorandir scrawled an amended version of my outburst into the box. Then he stood and returned the clipboard and the half-chewed pen to the reception desk. The receptionist took it without looking at him and started pressing keys on her computer. She told us to go through to the waiting room.

"How long do you think it will be?"

"It'll take as long as it takes," the lady replied in a weary voice.

"Well, thank you for your help, Irene." At the mention of her name, the lady looked up and met Lorandir's green eyes. I could see the slight blush appear on her cheeks and her lips parted slightly as she took in his handsome face. She softened slightly and licked her lips.

"You're in luck, it's before the evening rush so I'd say it won't be too long love," her eyes narrowed as she focused on Errol, now dozing on the elf's shoulders, "but no pets in the A&E." I smiled at the speed with which she had returned to her bulldog receptionist self. Even elven charm didn't work for long on receptionists.

Lorandir walked back to me unabashed and pointed through another set of sliding doors to the waiting area, "Will you be alright? I'll just go and tie Errol up outside."

"You can't do that! He'll feel lonely."

The elf sighed, "OK, I'll call someone to come and pick him up. Will you be alright by yourself until then?"

"Don't even worry about it, Irene said it would be quick. I'll be in and out before you know it."

Lorandir looked dubious and he kissed me softly before taking out his phone and retreating outside. I squared my shoulders and stepped into the waiting area. Electric lights buzzed on the ceiling, despite the daylight streaming through the windows. The room was painted white, and the floor was some sort of weird grey plastic. Easy to wipe down, I guessed. I picked a plastic chair from the rows screwed to the floor in long benches. It was in the corner, away from other patients. I struggled to get comfortable on the hard seat and prepared for a long wait. I wished I still had coffee in my reusable cup and looked around for a machine.

One sat against the wall, its light blinking on and off and a large hand-written out of order sign stuck to it. No coffee then. I fidgeted on the seat, trying to get comfortable, and took in the other patients. There were five of us by the looks of it: the little boy with his injured leg happily playing on a handheld console, an elderly man bundled up in a large khaki green coat and apparently sleeping, two young women with wonky tiaras and a lot of make-up sat in one corner taking selfies, and two young people who I pegged as university students held hands tightly in adjacent seats.

The students returned my gaze and lifted their joined hands up. "Glued together," one of them said with a lopsided grin.

"Bloody magic glue!" added the other, pushing dark black hair out of his face with his free hand.

"You're the one who wanted to try it!"

"How was I supposed to know that everlasting meant it wouldn't come unstuck? I thought it was just a gimmick!"

"I'm never going out with you again!"

I checked the time on my phone. Three p.m. These two were doing nothing to help the student stereotype. I held up my finger to interrupt their argument. In the harsh electric lighting, it looked a worse shade of blue. "Pictsie bite."

"Nasty! I read a story about someone who got bitten by one of them last year."

"What happened?" I leaned forward.

"Went into a coma and died in the end. Weeks of agony first though, so the paper said…" the student trailed off.

Schiztz. I examined my finger again. Was it just my imagination or was the blue colour spreading down my hand? I tried to distract myself by picking up an old magazine someone had left on a plastic table. I was halfway through an article about a woman who had left her husband for his twin brother when a man walked through the waiting room, heading for the exit and holding a see-through plastic bag. It contained a vibrating phone.

"I still don't know how it got up there!" he said to a nurse. The medic kept a professional neutral expression on her face as he left the premises. She exchanged a wad of paperwork with the receptionist and called out a name. The football mum stood up, dragging her son up with her. She manoeuvred him expertly around the plastic chairs while his eyes stayed glued to the small screen in front of him. I turned my attention back to the magazine.

"Ame! Are you alright?" I jumped at my best friend's familiar voice and looked up just in time to see Aloora bound across the grey-ish floor and embrace me in a fierce hug. I let out an involuntary gasp of pain as her leather satchel bounced off my finger. Immediately, the small gnome released me. She frowned down at my blue flesh and grabbed my wrist. She twisted my hand this way and that, her eyes ablaze with curiosity.

"What are you doing here?"

"Making sure you're alright of course. Lorandir said you were poisoned."

I gawked at her. My best friend could drive, but she didn't have a car. I wondered if she'd borrowed her workplace's magical van to get here. As if she could read my thoughts, she carried on, "He rang Marco to collect Errol and I was in the flat. Of course, I was going to come and see you. You don't look too good." She squinted at my face.

I frowned at her. My finger was blue, sure, but I was fairly confident the rest of me was just how I looked on a hot day. "Where's Marco?" I asked after our Italian friend who shared our flat in Cardiff Bay.

"He's in the waiting zone outside. Errol got in as soon as he took down that horrible air freshener. I'll stay here with you..." My friend hesitated. I knew she longed to get back to whichever of her studies had kept her indoors on this beautiful day. My money was on her doctoral thesis on dragons and their use of language; it was due this year.

Lorandir arrived and took the seat next to me, "It's alright, I'll stay with her. It could be a long wait and Marco needs a hand with Errol."

Aloora looked me up and down, "OK, if you're sure…" She had obviously decided I wasn't at death's door and her studies were more urgent. She unlatched her leather satchel and stuffed a chocolate bar into my sweaty palm. "This'll keep you going, and I'll order something for when you're back. Call me as soon as you know anything."

The gnome hugged me again and then flounced out of the room. The university students stared after her, entranced by her stripy figure-hugging dress and oversized boots. I didn't have the heart to tell them that she batted for the other team.

Instead, I fumbled with my phone, swearing as I got the code wrong with my left hand before finally unlocking it. I texted Marco thanks for looking after Errol and told him there was a bag of coal in my room. With a full stomach, the small wyrm was likely to curl up and sleep for the rest of the day so he wouldn't be any trouble for my flatmates. Then I started scrolling through social media.

I was partway through a thread about which superhero would win in various scenarios while Lorandir went in search of a working coffee machine, when a group of rugby players came in. They were still in their grass-stained kits and laughing at a large full back, who had a dazed expression. I caught the whiff of alcohol from their breath as they sat uncomfortably close to the corner I had chosen. I tried to ignore them, but it was difficult when they started passing a rugby ball across the waiting room. One of them fumbled the pass and the odd-shaped ball sailed towards me. I held up my hands. Too late. The ball hit me smack in the face. Hard.

"Dzrak!" I swore. The ball bounced off my forehead and rolled under a seat nearby.

"Sorry."

I looked up at the sheepish six-foot four rugby player with a black eye and cauliflower ears. His gaze moved down to my chest. I pursed my lips. Corset tops were not a great choice for hospital waiting rooms with drunk men.

"What are you doing here then?" he asked as he sank into the vacant seat next to me.

I held up my finger to show him. Schiztz. The swelling looked bigger to me. When was I going to get seen? Wasn't magical poisoning urgent?

"Dave over there got himself a concussion," the bulky sportsman continued, ignoring my unnaturally coloured finger.

"I thought it was the off season?"

"Yeah, we were playing a friendly match for charity to keep up the fitness." I took in his large belly sceptically. He didn't notice, "And of course a few bevvies afterwards. Then Dave here decided to run straight into a wall. Didn't ya? You plonker!" The player stood up, pointed at Dave, and started a chant to a half-familiar tune. "What a plonker! What a plonker!" The rest of the rugby team joined in and surrounded Dave, pointing at him and giving him friendly punches on the arm. Dave grinned like he wasn't sure what was going on but was happy to be part of it. The chant continued but the player next to me sat down again and shrugged like I'd asked him a question.

"We thought we'd better bring him in just to be sure. I didn't fancy bringing him back to his missus without a clean bill of health."

I nodded weakly, feeling sorry for Dave.

The receptionist marched over. She placed her hands on her hips and had a look on her bulldog face that said enough was enough. "I'm going to have to ask all of you to leave! Now!"

"We can't leave him; he's had a head injury."

"One of you can stay. Everyone else out!"

"How's that for NHS treatment, hey?"

"I pay my taxes, you know!"

"You're unemployed!"

"Yeah, well, if I wasn't I'd pay my taxes!"

The rugby team formed a small huddle and eventually decided that one of them was sober enough to stay with Dave. The rest of them headed out to continue the after party. I heard cheers and another drunken chant burst out as they left the building.

Lorandir walked back in with two steaming cups of instant coffee. He looked at the bruise forming on my forehead and put the drinks down on one of the low plastic topped tables screwed to the floor. The elf knelt on the floor in front of me and pushed a loose strand of hair away from my face so he could examine my darkening skin. He shook his head and allowed a small burst of his magic to brush over my face. I relaxed against his hand as I enjoyed the familiar sensation of his healing energy.

"Amethyst Haernson, you attract more trouble than anyone I know." I smiled at him sheepishly and he continued, "These months with you have been the most alive I have ever felt, and I never want it to end. Will you do me the honour of being my life partner?"

Chapter 3

I stared at him. Had he just proposed? Holy dzrakballs.

"Are you sure?" I blurted out. I was still unable to believe that this gorgeous creature was my boyfriend, let alone that he might want to marry me. Plus, it was pretty surreal, being proposed to in a waiting room. Maybe I was hallucinating. Maybe the poison had caused me to pass out, and I was having a crazy dream.

The elf gave me a dazzling smile. "Of course I'm sure." Then his smile started to waver, "But I understand if it's too soon…if you don't want…"

Schiztz. He was normally so confident that it took me a moment to place his expression. He was worried I'd say no. I threw my arms around his neck, "Yes, of course it's a yes! Of course I choose you!"

The rest of the patients in the waiting room gave a loud cheer. If we'd been in a restaurant, there would have been the pop of a champagne cork. As it was, there was a loud buzz and then a doctor shouted my name. He looked about twelve. He held his clipboard like it was a shield and looked around the room with a confused expression. I guess his patients weren't normally this enthusiastic. I patted Lorandir on the back, wincing as I caught my own finger. We stood and walked over to the doctor. Everyone looked at us with broad grins. They seemed to be expecting something. I gave a shy wave as we went, a huge smile spread across my face. Another cheer went round the room. The students lifted their stuck hands in some sort of salute. I smiled up at Lorandir as we followed the doctor to a small room.

"We just got engaged," I felt I had to offer some sort of explanation and I couldn't seem to stop smiling.

"Congratulations. I'm Dr Singh. Now if you can sit on that chair and explain what the problem is." The doctor slipped straight into clinical mode, flicking through the pieces of paper attached to a clipboard instead of looking at his patient. He nodded along as I explained that I had been bitten by a pictsie and my finger was now swollen and blue. I held up the offending appendage. He ignored me and instead reeled off a list of questions about potential symptoms. I said no to everything.

No, I hadn't been unconscious since the bite. No, I didn't have a headache, although the electric lighting was starting to grate on me. He didn't laugh.

No, I didn't have chest pains or shortness of breath. And so on. He took my blood pressure and my temperature and made more notes on a chart in front of him. Finally, he asked to see my finger. He regarded it with some professional curiosity and then squeezed it gently.

"Ow!"

"Does that hurt?"

"Yes!"

"How long ago were you bitten?"

"Er, a couple of hours, I guess."

His dark brows drew together in confusion, "Where is the wound?"

I looked down at my finger and then at Lorandir. He shrugged, "I healed it."

Dr Singh blinked three times as he studied the elf. I could almost hear him going through a mental checklist. Pointy ears. Tall. Gorgeous. Elf.

"Fascinating," was the closest he allowed himself to get to enthusiasm, "I wonder if you've heard of our magical healing clinic? We're working with magical beings to study their powers more closely with the aim of melding modern science and spells together for better healing."

"I had heard that there were some trials being started." That was news to me. Although it was nice to hear mundane and magical beings were working together, maybe that would ease some of the friction which had seemed to escalate between the two species since dragons had appeared in the world.

"I wonder if you'd be interested at all…" Lorandir hesitated, but the doctor pushed on, "I'll find you a leaflet."

"Er, my finger?"

"Yes, well, pictsies are venomous and so should really be avoided," his brown eyes hardened as he looked at me, "it's not as fast moving as snake venom and you don't seem to have any symptoms of severe poisoning. Fortunately, we carry a stock of antivenin here thanks to a number of bites this summer. The critters seem to have been more active than usual and have spread outside of their usual Cornish habitat." I nodded along. "So, we'll have to give you an IV with the antivenin and a rabies injection." He scrawled something on the notes before leading me out of the room and along the corridor to a ward. There were six beds, all with those flimsy hospital curtains attached to plastic rails surrounding them. Two were empty. The doctor gestured to one, and I climbed in. The blanket was itchy against my bare arms.

A nurse joined us, wheeling a metal pole with a hook attached to it. She studied the form the doctor handed her and gave a nod before heading off to find the right IV bag. Another nurse bustled in and asked for my arm. I eyed him suspiciously as he unwrapped a needle.

"Just giving you the anti-rabies injection," he prodded me with a needle. I shrieked. He ignored me and carried on, "and now I'm just fitting a cannula for you, slight scratch…"

I swore. Slight scratch my ass. He inserted a long needle just below my inner elbow.

"You've got good veins," he smiled at me. I gritted my teeth and nodded. I took after my Dad in a lot of ways and having veins that were easy to find was one of them. He always joked it was his hot dwarven blood.

The first nurse arrived back with a bag of fluid. It had a silhouette of a pictsie on it, wings and all, and a lot of medical words. She attached it to the hook on the metal pole and then allowed the liquid to flow into a long tube. She held the transparent tube up to the light and studied it for a few seconds before connecting it to the contraption now embedded in my arm. I felt the cool liquid enter my veins before my body acclimatised. Satisfied that I was hooked up, they all turned to leave.

"So, when can I go home?"

Dr Singh turned back to me. He looked at the older, more experienced nurses for help, but they had gone to their next patients. He sighed and fiddled with the pen in his pocket, "I'd like to keep you in overnight for observation…" I stared at him. He looked up, then down, then at me with another sigh, "But if you're stable when the IV drip is finished, I suppose you can go."

"Thank you," I settled back onto the bed. With a nod, the doctor scurried off.

"Can I get you anything?" Lorandir fluffed my pillows then hovered by the bed. It was sweet. I smiled at him, remembering we were engaged.

"Any chance of a coffee?"

While he went off to find a machine, my phone rang. I saw Gunther's name appear on the screen. Why was my supplier calling me at the weekend? I tried to think if I'd placed any unusual orders recently that he might be updating me on as I answered the phone clumsily, wincing as my movement wiggled the needle stuck into my arm.

"Hey Gunther."

"How's my favourite client?" I was fairly sure Gunther greeted all of his clients like that, but he was my Dad's friend and the best supplier of jewels and metals in the city so I wasn't about to call him on it.

"Is anything wrong?" I thought of the workbench he was loaning me in his warehouse. Maybe something had happened there.

"Nothing's wrong…"

"But?"

"You've had a letter delivered here…"

"And?"

"It's from the Dwarven Arms Council."

"Schiztz." Good things rarely came from the Council. Especially not for half-dwarves. The first time I'd made it onto their radar, they'd threatened to take away my ancestral axe. My hand went instinctively to my side. I knew I shouldn't have left my weapon at home.

"Do you want to come and get it?" Gunther was more curious than me about the letter.

I looked at the IV bag. The level of clear liquid had barely moved. "I can't right now. I'm in hospital." I'd spoken without thinking and regretted it immediately.

"What?! Are you alright? Do your parents know?"

"I was about to text them; I've only just got treated. It's all fine, don't even worry about it. Just a pictsie bite."

"They're nasty pests, they are. How did you get bitten? I thought they were afraid of people."

I thought back to the evil glittering eyes as the creature had sunk its teeth into me, "Yeah well, this one wasn't."

"I'll bring it to yours then, shall I?"

"Don't worry about it, I'm not sure when I'll be out of here, it could be a few hours," I eyed the bag angrily, willing its contents to hurry up and get inside me. "I'll pick it up on Monday."

"Amethyst! You know better than that! It's from the Dwarven Arms Council, it can't wait until Monday. Come over tomorrow."

"Will your warehouse be open on a Sunday?" Stupid question.

"I never close. See you tomorrow."

Chapter 4

The driver let us out just outside my apartment block in Cardiff Bay. It was a nice area, a short walk from the regenerated waterfront brasseries and bars. The sort of area I couldn't have afforded if we weren't splitting the rent three ways and getting a sizeable discount thanks to last year's dragon scare. A faint thrum of music pounded the air as we got out of the car and walked towards the building. People were still enjoying a weekend party by the sounds of it.

We took the lift up to the flat I shared with Aloora and Marco. I'd insisted on sleeping in my own bed tonight. I wanted to make sure Errol was alright and Lorandir's penthouse was lovely, but I didn't think I'd left any clean clothes there. The elevator shuddered to a stop on our floor, and I stomped across the carpeted hallway to our flat.

I fumbled with the key. My finger had deflated a little, but it was still swollen. Inside, I found Marco and Aloora watching a film. I walked over and plopped myself down onto an upcycled armchair. The fabric was soft, and the chair was comfy, even if it was a hideous shade of orange. I motioned for them to pass over the popcorn. I was starving. Lorandir sank to the floor next to me. I handed him a cushion and he arranged his long body comfortably before leaning against my legs. As I crammed the caramelised kernels into my face, they paused the film and began firing questions.

"How are you?"

I lifted my hand. My finger was now a pale eggshell blue, and the doctor was confident the antivenin had worked. He had still wanted to keep me in for observations but had let me go after Lorandir had promised to get me straight back to the hospital if there were any changes to my condition. The doctor was still a bit in awe of the elf's healing powers and had stuffed a leaflet about the trial into his hand as we left.

"'Ow did that creature bite you?"

I shrugged, "I tried to rescue it from the road, and it turned on me. Dzraking pictsies. How's Errol?"

Aloora shifted on the sofa to show my pet wyrm curled up between her and Marco. He was fast asleep.

"'E is no trouble," Marco confirmed.

Aloora got up to make a hot drink.

"How's your essay going?" I shouted through to the kitchen.

Marco narrowed his eyes at a pile of paperwork that had escaped from Aloora's room and had colonised one of his upcycled tabletops. The paper completely hid the shabby chic finish he'd spent a week applying to the piece.

"OK, I'm meeting with the Professor this week and I want to have something decent to show him. I shouldn't really have changed my topic so late into the programme, but it was too good an opportunity to pass up on…"

"She told me she would film me sleeping and put it online if I touched her work. I only want to tidy up. It is like, 'ow you say, a pigsty in here!"

I tried not to laugh at Marco's indignation. I knew Aloora's room was an absolute state of papers, scrolls, and books. This pile was the tip of the iceberg. But it jarred with Marco's tidiness. I wondered how he had stayed in his previous student house share for so long. That kitchen had been a breeding ground for all types of germs.

"What else have you been up to?" I tried to smooth over the tension.

"Not much," Aloora returned with two mugs of steaming tea and handed them to me and Lorandir. I sniffed. Peppermint. My gnomish friend caught my expression, "It's good for you."

"Thank you Aloora," Lorandir had better manners than me. I echoed him and raised my mug in a sarcastic salute to my friend. "Shall we tell them?" he whispered to me.

I reached down and held his hand. The proposal in the waiting room seemed like it had happened a long time ago.

"Er, yes, me and Lorandir have got some news…"

My flatmates looked at me curiously. I felt my face heat as I became the centre of attention. Despite my confidence that we had chosen each other, I didn't know how to say it, so I blurted it out in one go. "LorandirandIareengaged."

Aloora looked from me to the elf sitting at my feet. His ears had flushed a slight pink, his equivalent of a blush, but he had a huge smile on his face. She screamed and rushed over to hug me and then him. Marco still had a bemused look on his face.

"What is 'appening?"

"They're engaged! This is so exciting Ame! Where are you going to get married? Have you picked a date?" She screamed again, "I get to plan your hen do! This is so exciting!"

"No strippers!" Aloora laughed at me, but I was serious. My friend had a strange sense of humour sometimes, probably from spending too long cooped up with musty old books.

"We must celebrate!" Marco headed to the fridge and pulled out a bottle of prosecco. He uncorked it like a pro and found four mismatched champagne flutes I hadn't realised we owned in the top of a cupboard. He handed them round and we toasted our engagement.

"About time!" Aloora added to her toast. I looked at her questioningly. "I knew you were going to end up together forever. It's so damn romantic. So where are you going to get married then?"

I blinked and took a sip of the chilled wine. The bubbles tickled my nose and made me sneeze. That gave me some cover. I hadn't really had time to process the practicalities of an actual wedding. I was just happy that Lorandir loved me and wanted to spend the rest of our lives together. Schiztz. Well, the rest of my life. He probably had another couple of hundred years left. My sneezing fit passed and Aloora was still waiting for a reply.

"Er, I think we're just going to enjoy our engagement for a bit before we have a ceremony."

Lorandir nodded along with my hastily created cover story. His eyes were wide. I guessed we had a lot to talk about.

"Where is the ring?" Marco grabbed my hand and studied it carefully. I pulled it away. My index finger was still sore.

"I didn't get one," Lorandir took some pressure off me by replying, "Amethyst is so precise about her jewellery, I didn't want to get her anything she might not like. I thought we could have fun finding a ring together." I smiled at the elf. He really did know me.

I had eclectic tastes when it came to jewellery. My eyes found Aloora's collar necklace sitting easily around her throat. It was my favourite piece and the best work I had done, setting a genuine dragon scale into hammered gold. I definitely wanted to choose my own engagement ring…or maybe make my own.

My eyes glazed over as I started playing with designs inside my head. A diamond was classic, but was it too cliché? I could use elven steel as a nod to my fiancé…

"How did your Dad react?" Aloora's question brought me back to earth. Schiztz, I hadn't told my parents yet.

"Er…I'd better call them," I pulled out my phone and the display glared at me accusingly. It was after midnight. I had had several texts through from Mum since I'd told them I was in hospital. The last one was thirty minutes ago. I squeezed Lorandir's hand, then I stepped into my bedroom and took a deep breath.

Mum picked up after the second ring, "Ame! Darling, are you OK?"

"Er yes Mum, I'm fine, I'm out of hospital now. Doctor says I'm alright."

"Have you had any headaches? Any numbness around the bite? Any trouble breathing?"

"Mum! I was checked out at the hospital, honestly stop reading things on the internet. I am fine."

"Alright, alright, don't bite my head off. I just want to know my baby is OK so I can get some sleep! Honestly!"

"Is Dad there?"

"Your father's here and he's been under my feet all evening. Here, you talk to him."

"Amethyst! Not dead then?" Dad's face appeared on my phone screen next to Mum. He had worked his beard into multiple plaits, always a sign he was worrying about something.

"Not yet! Er, there's something I want to tell you…LorandirandIareengaged." That was the second time I'd spit out the words as fast as possible.

"What was that love? The signal went a bit funny." Dad tapped at the screen.

"Lorandir and I are engaged!" I practically shouted at the phone. The screen went dark. I heard a scuffle and mumbled words.

"Sorry about that darling, your father just dropped the phone. That's wonderful news! We'll have to come to Cardiff to celebrate, won't we Dafydd?" The slight grunt from my Dad made me wonder if Mum had elbowed him in the ribs.

"Yes, yes, good news. He's a lovely…elf. You're sure…oof," another jab from Mum, "I mean I'm proud of you love. Where is he then?"

I opened the door and gestured to Lorandir. He was talking to his cousin on his own phone. We swapped.

"Congratulations!" King Morthimas' voice was cheerful as he smiled in the small screen. I smiled back. At least he was taking it well. In the background, I could hear Dad mumbling something to my fiancé. "And, of course, you can have the wedding here, after all it's Lorandir's home." My attention snapped back to the King.

"Er…we haven't exactly decided where…" I had no doubts at all about what Dad would say about his daughter getting married in an elven city. I tuned into the other conversation in time to hear my Dad say, "…have the ceremony in Jarnstradr."

"Er…got to go Morty, speak soon." I hung up and hurried over to Lorandir's side at the mention of the dwarven city. "We only got engaged tonight! We haven't made any arrangements yet!"

"No, of course you haven't love, I was just saying it's a lovely place."

"Well, we'd better go, let you enjoy your first night together as an affianced couple!" Mum winked down the phone and raised a glass. Both my parents had glasses of champagne in their hands. That was fast work. "Congratulations! To you both." Mum added meaningfully. Their faces disappeared.

I turned to Lorandir. What had we done? Organising a wedding between a half-dwarf and an elven sort of prince was going to be difficult.

Chapter 5

I woke up to a watery sun streaming through my bedroom window. Unsurprisingly, Lorandir was already awake. He put down the dog-eared fantasy novel he'd taken from my crowded shelves and gave me a dazzling smile.

"Morning fiancée."

"Morning fiancé," I rubbed my eyes, a stupid grin on my own face.

Despite the strangeness of yesterday, it was nice to have our relationship more official. I'd always felt slightly awkward going out with someone so attractive and tall and related to royalty, so it was reassuring that he wanted more. I wanted to ask what his own parents had said when he'd called them, but his lips claimed mine before I could speak. It wasn't until much later that morning, while we were having brunch perched on the tall stools in the small kitchenette, that I could ask him.

He concentrated on his plate of eggs. Omelettes were the one thing I could make, and I'd flavoured them with pepper and earthy aromatic Mucklewhite mushrooms that had survived both my half-hearted attempts to care for them and a fire at my shop. They were hardy and they tasted good.

"They're happy that I am happy," Lorandir replied carefully. I gave him a look. "Well, Mother wasn't exactly thrilled that there's going to be a dwarf in the family, but she didn't disown me, so she'll come around."

"Sounds like her views are similar to my Dad's."

He blanched suddenly, "I don't think Mother would threaten you."

"What? When did Dad threaten you?" I thought back to last night. There had been a small amount of time when I'd let Lorandir speak to my parents unsupervised. Schiztz. "What did he say?"

"Not much, just that if I ever hurt you, he'd hunt me down with a gang of his mates."

"He didn't?!"

"I'm paraphrasing. I didn't understand all of the curse words he used," there was a glint of humour in his bright green eyes. I was going to have to talk to Dad. Lorandir leaned back on the stool and stretched, something that only an elf could attempt without falling over. "So, what shall we do today?"

"I dunno, what do you want to do?"

"We've already done what I wanted to do…" he gave me a slow self-satisfied smile. I threw a tea towel at his chest. He let it hit him with a laugh.

"Oh schiztz, I've got to pop into Gunther's warehouse. There's some sort of letter for me…from the Dwarven Arms Council," I grimaced and took a sip of my milky coffee.

Aloora wandered out of her room, her short hair spiking out in all directions. She rubbed her eyes. "Why are you being so loud so early in the morning?"

"It's gone eleven o'clock!"

She waved away my comment and poured herself a smoothie from the fridge before sitting down on the remaining stool.

"Do you want me to make you an omelette?"

She shook the smoothie at me. It was green and smelled like freshly mown grass. "No thanks, you use too much butter."

"That's what makes it so good," I used the last of the eggs to mop the tomato ketchup from my plate before stuffing the forkful into my mouth. Suitably fed, Lorandir and I got dressed and I prodded Errol awake with my toe.

"Come on boy, let's go for a walk." Errol tried to rollover and go back to sleep but I had promised Uncle Owain I would keep him healthy.

Gunther's warehouse was on an industrial estate on the outskirts of the city. Recently, I'd invested in a bicycle in an effort to save money; the bus fares or taxi fees from here to the city weren't cheap. Of course, I still took the bus when it rained. Or when it was too cold. Or if I felt like it. Another upside was that the regular exercise was meant to tighten up my curves. Although it might work better if I wasn't only cycling sporadically.

I dragged the bike into the lift along with the small wyrm. Lorandir followed us in. The lift stopped two floors down and a lady with a buggy and two small children stared at me for taking up the entire space. I muttered an apology and stabbed at the button to close the doors. Once outside in the warm air, I strapped on my black helmet and wobbled onto my bike. Lorandir offered to take Errol's lead and jog beside me. His long stride easily kept pace with my frantic pedalling.

Fortunately, the traffic wasn't too heavy today, it being Sunday, and we made it to the industrial estate with only one car cutting me up on the way. I gave it the finger without taking my hands off the handlebars and kept going. I was sweaty and out of breath as I pulled up outside Gunther's warehouse and chained up my bike.

No one would be stupid enough to steal from the dwarf's business, but I tried to keep in the habit of locking up my front wheel in case I forgot to do it when I biked into the city centre.

Lorandir waited until I'd finished before holding open the door to Gunther's office for me. He followed me in, and I went straight through to the poky kitchen for a glass of water. Lorandir didn't even look out of breath after his long run, but he accepted a glass anyway. I downed my drink and refilled it.

"Well, well, look what the cat dragged in."

I turned to see a green-skinned kobold leaning against the doorframe, "Hi Bethan, is Gunther around?"

"Not my job to keep an eye on the boss," she shrugged. "We're all interested in what the Arms Council has to say to you though. I offered to open it…but he insisted we leave it for you."

"Where's the letter then?"

"With the boss," she smiled infuriatingly. I pushed past her. "Try the workbenches," she called after me.

I stomped towards the benches. There was a goblin behind one holding up jewels and making notes in a leather-bound ledger set up on the table in front of him. My own bench was close-by. I ran my hand over the surface, feeling the usual calm that filled me before I started creating. Gunther had provided me with a small safe to keep my pieces in while I didn't have a shop.

I thought about the collection I was creating stored inside it; Out of the Ashes. It was my way of dealing with the fire that had consumed my shop in a popular Cardiff Arcade. I used copper and red and yellow stones to create flame-like rings and necklaces. My hands itched to get back to work with the metals.

My next challenge was creating a bracelet that looked like a dragon encircling the wrist. I mused over whether to add a small ruby in as its eye and what the best setting would be.

And I still had to decide on a ring. Did I want to make it myself or buy one? I rubbed my forehead. There was too much to think about. Errol padded across the floor and collapsed under my bench. He started snoring almost instantly, tired out from the long jog.

"Ho! Amethyst! There you are!"

I turned at the sound of Gunther's booming voice. He sported a long-sleeved shirt and an embroidered waistcoat. The only concession he made to the heat was rolling his shirtsleeves up to his elbows. I clasped his forearm in the traditional dwarven greeting.

"I hear congratulations are in order!" Gunther pulled me forward into a hug. I tried not to breathe in his beard at the unexpected embrace. He released me and gave Lorandir a similar hug. "This calls for a celebration! Come on, and I've got your letter in the office, where it's safe from prying eyes."

He led the way into his cramped office and flipped on a fan. It moved the warm air around the room and rustled the piles of papers. The dwarf pulled out three shot glasses from somewhere and filled them with an amber coloured liquid from a misshapen glass bottle. I took the glass cautiously and gave it a sniff. Fire whisky.

Gunther said congratulations again and tipped the whisky down his throat before smacking his lips with relish. I followed suit.

The best thing to do with the dwarven drink is to get it down you before you get too much of the taste on your tongue. It's called fire whisky for a reason. I felt the magic-imbued alcohol reacting with my saliva and swallowed it down my throat with only a small cloud of smoke escaping from my mouth with a cough. Gunther laughed and slapped my back. I smiled back then looked at Lorandir.

The elf sniffed the whisky delicately. "It smells like sulphur and chilli peppers and…something else."

"Best not to think about it too much lad, just get it down you!"

Lorandir swallowed and then tilted the glass to his mouth. His eyes bulged as he felt the burning sensation of the fire whisky reacting with saliva. Unfortunately, Gunther clapped him on the back at the same time and instead of swallowing the dangerous liquor, Lorandir sprayed it across the room in a large fireball.

Gunther shouted and began hitting at the small flames that had started where the liquid had touched neatly stacked invoices. Bethan flung the door open and sprayed all three of us with white foam from a fire extinguisher. She ignored the small fires on Gunther's desk and focused on us as he patted out the flames. The stream of foam finished. The kobold kept her hand pressed down on the trigger until the extinguisher gave one final spurt. She looked like she was enjoying this a lot.

"Yes, thank you Bethan, if you would be so kind as to get us a towel…" Gunther glared at her as he slapped out the last flame on his desk. With a smirk, the kobold left to find a towel.

Gunther took a final swig of fire whisky before he corked the bottle and set it down next to his computer. I could sense the enchantments on the metal stopper and the patterned glass, designed to keep the volatile liquid contained. With a flourish, Gunther stopped rooting around in the paperwork and presented me with a folded piece of parchment. It was slightly singed in one corner and now had a damp patch where Gunther's foam-covered hands had touched it. I recognised the large wax seal holding it shut. There was no mistaking the Dwarven Arms Council's crest; an axe and a mining pickaxe crossed over a mining helmet.

I tried in vain to wipe my own hands down before I touched it, but only succeeded in moving the foam around my workout clothes. Bethan reappeared and flung a scrap of towel at each of us. I dried my hands carefully and took the proffered parchment.

With mounting trepidation, I broke the seal. My palms were suddenly sweaty, and my knees felt weak. I opened the thick paper; my hands trembled so much it was difficult to make out the words. I walked back out of the office and over to my workbench, dripping globs of foam onto the concrete floor as I went. Back at the safety of my bench, I laid the parchment down and weighted either side with a couple of my tools before gripping the surface for support. My mouth dropped open.

Lorandir appeared behind me and placed his hands on my shoulders, "Whatever it is, we'll handle it together."

I heard Gunther's boots clopping against the concrete, "Well Amethyst, what does it say?"

Speechless, I pointed to the curly text:

Ms Amethyst Haernson, your attendance is required at the Halls of the Dwarven Arms Council at ten o'clock a.m. on the twentieth of September, in order that you may receive from the Council, the Medal of Honour for your bravery in the Battle of Avalon. You may be accompanied by up to four companions and I shall be glad if you will complete the enclosed form and return it to the Council immediately. This letter should be produced on entering the Halls as no further cards of admission will be issued.

It was signed by Master Ironfist with a flourish and followed by a personal note:

"Dzrak me!" Gunther swore behind me, "That's a great honour. I haven't known the Council to give out a medal in fifty years! Well done, Amethyst!"

"But I didn't do anything!" I protested.

My mind went back to that day not so long ago in the fae realm when Mordred had attacked Avalon, hoping to conquer it. I had been absent from the battle, instead serving as a lookout for the troops on the ground. My fighting skills weren't on a par with any of the other warriors there.

I mean, yes, I had got into hand-to-hand combat with Mordred when he flew a dragon over the castle walls and everyone else was out fighting his horde of nightmare creatures, but it wasn't like I'd defeated him.

He was on the brink of killing me when Aloora had flown a dzraking dragon through a stained-glass window. I shook my head guiltily; I did not deserve any honours from the Council. "I'll have to turn it down!"

Gunther pulled his beard, "Turn it down! What would your father say?!"

I stared at the paper as Lorandir squeezed my shoulder reassuringly. I knew exactly what my father, the master craftsdwarf, would say if he found out his daughter had turned down one of the highest honours in dwarfdom. It wouldn't be pretty.

With a sigh, I dug out a pen and filled out the form attached to the bottom of the parchment. As soon as I'd finished, the form section tore itself free from the paper and began to fold in on itself.

I took a step back and watched as it folded itself neatly into halves, then quarters, then eighths, sixteenths and thirty-seconds. It kept going until it vanished with a small pop. I rubbed at the small black smudge it had left on the workbench. I guess we were going to the largest dwarven city in the UK to collect a dzraking medal.

Chapter 6

"What do you want to do now?" Lorandir pulled me from my reverie.

"Go into town and eat cake." It wasn't the best plan in the world, but it sounded good to me. I waved off Gunther's offer of more celebratory drinks and ignored Bethan's smug smile. The elf bundled Errol, still sleeping, into the small basket on my bike, and we set off to the city centre.

It was only as we got close to the Dragon's Head, my favourite coffee shop, that I realised Brinda closed early on a Sunday. Schiztz. Instead, we went to the black-beamed Rummer Tavern and squeezed into the last remaining table. I thought about the medal. It was an honour, sure, but I had a bad feeling about it.

"Are you going to tell your Dad?"

Schiztz. Two calls in less than twenty-four hours. My parents were going to think something was seriously wrong. Dad picked up Mum's phone when I called.

"Hello love, to what do we owe the pleasure?"

I heard bubbles in the background and took in Dad's wet beard. Schiztz. They were in the hot tub. "Er…"

Dad's face darkened, "If that elf has so much as hurt you…but you're better off without him, you know. You can do better; I know a few dwarves who might be interested…"

"Dad! I'm still engaged to Lorandir! He's here with me now!"

"Oh. Hi Lorandir, glad everything's OK. So, what's happened, love? You look terrible."

"Er, I got a message from the Dwarven Arms Council today…"

"Those stuffed shirts! They keep sending me all their troublemakers to teach, I swear if they've been talking about your axe again, I've half a mind to march to their bloody hall and…"

I cut him off, "No Dad, it's nothing like that. They've invited me to receive a medal of honour."

Dad's face went blank before bursting into a huge grin, "Dzraking hell Amethyst! The first Haernson to receive a medal of honour since your great grandad saved that mine. And you'll get yours in person, not posthumously! Here, talk to your mother." He passed over the phone and I repeated the news to Mum.

"That's fantastic news! They say good things come in threes; you ought to buy a lottery ticket too!"

I heard the sound of a cork popping and Dad's face swam back into view, "So when's the date? I'll have to polish up my chainmail."

I gave him the details, "I can only bring four companions though."

"Well of course we'll be there, who else are you bringing?"

"Er, Lorandir…"

"An elf?!" Dad spat out his mouthful of champagne. I briefly wondered how many bottles of the stuff they had on ice.

"Of course, she's taking her fiancé, Dafydd! Stop being ridiculous."

Dad muttered something under his breath. I cut across him not sure I wanted to hear his thoughts on an elf in the largest dwarven city in Britain, "And maybe Aloora, or Uncle Owain. I haven't decided yet."

"Of course you haven't, darling. I'll have to come up to the city to help you choose an outfit." I tried not to grimace at Mum's words. She loved clothes shopping. I did not.

I said my goodbyes and just before I pressed the red button to hang up, I heard Dad say, "But an elf…" in a disappointed tone. It was too much to hope that my elven fiancé hadn't heard. His keen hearing was as good as Errol's when I'd opened a fresh pack of premium coal. I took his hand and gave it a squeeze. Dad would come round. Eventually…Probably…Maybe.

I spent the rest of the day calling up my dwarven relatives after Dad insisted I had to tell them in person. Fortunately, Dad had already broken the news about my engagement so half of them didn't even take my call and I could leave a message. It was the first time I'd been thankful for the prejudices of some of my older relatives.

Uncle Owain and his husband Dylan were over the top enthusiastic about both the engagement and the medal. It was a little forced, but I was happy that they took it in their stride.

Two days later, a parcel arrived stamped with a familiar dragon symbol that was the logo for my uncle's wyrm farm. I opened it to find a boozy fruit cake wrapped in brown paper; Dylan's specialty. It was moist and delicious, with delicate crunches of walnuts mixed among the plump raisins and cherries. It knocked Marco and Aloora out after one slice. Lorandir managed one and a half. I was more used to Dylan's overuse of alcohol in his cooking, but even I crashed and fell asleep on the sofa after two generous slices.

I awoke the next day slightly hungover and annoyed with myself; I should have known better than to go back for seconds of Dylan's fruitcake. I poured myself a glass of cola from the fridge.

At least my healthy flatmates were still spark out, so they couldn't admonish me for drinking the sugary drink first thing in the morning. I was halfway through the glass when my phone rang. I checked the screen. Mum. I took the call in my bedroom rather than disturb the three sleeping forms spread out in our lounge.

"They printed it!"

"What?"

"They printed it! It looks great. I had to use the picture from when you first met because you still haven't given me one of you two together, but I think it came out well. And you'll never guess what," Mum barrelled on without giving me the opportunity to guess, "the nationals are interested. They want to do a feature, isn't that amazing?!"

"Mum! Stop! I have no idea what you're talking about," my head was spinning.

"The paper, silly, I'm sure I told you. I sent in an announcement for your engagement, and they printed it." Mum waved a newspaper in front of the phone.

I squinted, trying to make out the article. It had a huge headline above a picture of me and Lorandir. My heart sank. It was the picture from the local Cardiff paper after the first dragon had awakened. I looked a mess, but at least I had an excuse; I had been tied up by a cult, knocked out and nearly killed. Typically, Lorandir still looked gorgeous in black and white, even with his singed hair.

"You didn't tell me Mum," it came out in a horrified whisper.

"I'm sure I did. Anyway, doesn't it look lovely? You made the front page as well! It's not every day a dwarf and an elf get engaged," she looked proudly at the article.

"Does it say I'm a dwarf?" I was suddenly anxious. The Dwarven Arms Council took a dim view of people pretending to be full-blooded dwarves, and I didn't want any trouble with them, especially when they were giving me a dzraking medal.

"Well, they may have got their facts wrong, but don't worry, your Dad's been on the phone and they'll be printing a correction tomorrow."

"How could you Mum?"

"How could I what?"

"How could you write into the paper like that? It's a complete invasion of privacy!"

"It's traditional to announce engagements! And excuse me for being proud of my daughter! I thought you'd want to shout your news to the world! What's wrong? Are you ashamed of Lorandir?"

"What?! Of course not!"

"All I ever want is to do the best for you, and you're so prickly…"

"OK, OK, sorry for snapping. Just don't put my name in the paper again, please?"

"Alright, but I think you're overreacting. This will be good for you; I mentioned your business and everything. Anyway, I was thinking of coming up next weekend. Now you don't have to be at a storefront every weekend, we can hit the town and do some shopping. You want to look your best, don't you? I've heard good things about the new John Lewis collection…"

"Sure, sure, whatever," I wasn't interested in hearing about the latest fashions. I already had my laptop open and was searching for the dzraking article. "What did you say the name of the paper was?"

Mum told me then signed off saying she was meeting friends for breakfast and Bellinis to celebrate her daughter being in the local paper. Not only had Mum ruined my day, but she was also using it to score points with her friends.

I found the article and started reading. Less than halfway through I groaned and made my way into the kitchen for my second glass of cola. I briefly considered adding vodka to it but changed my mind. I needed a clear head in case anyone else had read the dzraking article. At least it was only a small local paper.

That was before Aloora whirled into the kitchen with her head down, tapping at her phone screen.

"What's this?"

"Er…"

"Why didn't you tell me you were announcing the engagement? I would have asked for an exclusive for my online channel!"

"It was Mum, not me!"

That slightly mollified my friend. "OK, but I still want an exclusive. This is going viral. I'll set up my studio. Interview tonight. Right, got to go or I'll be late." With that, she swept out of the door to her job at the Magical Liaison Office.

I stood there gaping after her. Dzraking great.

Chapter 7

I paused in front of the wedding shop on Castle Street. Their display of dresses on slender mannequins did nothing to help my mood.

I looked down at the newspaper in my hand. Since doing the dzraking interview with Aloora, the media seemed to have gone crazy about our relationship.

I winced as I thought back to our unplanned responses to her questions. She had mainly focused on how we'd met, given that she was most interested in dragons, but that meant journalists could speculate on everything else.

Mum had brought me the latest daily paper, which had a double page spread on dwarf-elf relationships. Mine and Lorandir's engagement featured heavily.

Was this a new age for two traditionally warring species? asked the paper. Their description of me was both factually accurate and disparaging.

Amethyst Haernson (32) is a buxom half-dwarf who runs an online jewellery store since losing her storefront in a fire last year. She seems unassuming, but could this pint-sized dwarf heal the rift between two species? Since becoming engaged to

57

the handsome and highly eligible Prince Lorandir, a member of the elven royal family, the two have yet to make an official public appearance together, suggesting tension in the royal family. When asked for comment, an aide provided this statement, "We can confirm the engagement between Prince Lorandir and Amethyst Haernson. Prince Lorandir's duties to the royal family are unaffected by this engagement. A date for the wedding has yet to be set."

When pressed about a possible title, the aide confirmed, "There have been no discussions about whether Ms Haernson will be provided with a title, although it would be highly irregular for a dwarf to hold a title, given their republican society." A representative of the Dwarven Arms Council commented, "We hold no say over the private lives of individuals, let alone half-breeds. I don't know why you even called me."

Members of the public are divided on the issue. Mrs Smith (60) from Somerset thinks "It's beautiful, isn't it? A real-life fairy tale. I wish them every happiness and hope there's a big wedding." Others are not so happy, Miss Robtree (37) believes there's been foul play, "It's not right, is it? I mean, look at her and look at him. You can get all sorts of potions nowadays; I hope someone's looking into that."

Madam Mim (age not given), the leading purveyor of potions in the UK, was unavailable for comment, fuelling speculation that one of her love potions may have led Haernson to capture the heart of a prince. Sales of Mim's no. 9 love tincture are up by two hundred per cent according to one stockist...

Mr Lionel (54) from Kent suspects a more sinister motive, "The dwarves and elves are ganging up together now. I mean, what does that say about the state of the country and what does it mean for us normal folk? Mark my words, this is the start of an alliance I'll bet and then you'd better lock up your kids before they start eating them."

Both the Elven High Council and the Dwarven Arms Council vehemently denied their species ever ate human children. Gundersson (135), owner of a popular local delicatessen, confirmed that children weren't on the menu, "Why would we eat children? There's much nicer meats available; my special smoked sausage is on offer this week."

The paper had used not only the hideous picture of me and Lorandir covered in dust and grime but had somehow found pictures of the stylised dwarf Marco had painted in my shop before it had burnt down. I had hoped the fire had destroyed I for good, but the large-breasted dwarf-woman complete with leather, chainmail and a beard stared back at me from the paper.

I was so engrossed in the paper that it took me a minute to recognise the feeling that there was a dagger aimed at my back. Someone was staring at me. I turned around quickly.

The Cardiff streets were full of the usual mix of tourists, students, and shoppers. A group of youths in dark hoodies scrolled through their phones in front of the large statue of Aneurin Bevan that dominated one end of the main pedestrianised shopping area.

A mum pushed a buggy laden with so much shopping I could barely make out the chocolate-covered toddler sat in it. The toddler was busying itself with emptying a bag of clothes and dropping them onto the uneven paving one at a time. The mum hadn't noticed the trail of socks and pants on the floor.

Nothing out of the ordinary. I spun around slowly, my hand on the top of my double-headed axe. I'd started carrying it again for the illusion of comfort it gave me.

A small group of teenage girls eyed me. "Go on," one of them urged.

I frowned. Surely, they weren't the source of the malevolence I sensed. I stepped backwards as one of the gaggle approached me.

"You're her, aren't you?"

"Er…"

"Amethyst? The dwarf who's marrying a prince."

"Er…yes?"

"Can you sign this?" She thrust a piece of paper at me. Was I a celebrity now? I scribbled my name down and handed the paper back as the girls giggled about meeting a princess.

"Did you use a love potion?"

My mouth fell open. One of them, the one with the greasiest hair, and a top covered with bright pineapples looked me up and down. Her eyes paused on my stomach.

"Are you pregnant?"

I gaped at her. I mean, sure, I didn't have washboard abs, but my belly wasn't big enough to suggest a baby was hiding in there!

"Are you?" I snapped back.

She blinked at me, her dark eyebrows furrowing at my angry response. I mean, I was curvy, but come on! Before I could deny the rumour properly, I heard a polite cough behind me.

While I was distracted, a black limousine had pulled up nearby. An elegant, gloved hand reached out of the blackened window and beckoned me over. I pointed to myself with a look of confusion on my face, ignoring the girls who still tittered behind me. The lilac glove continued to beckon.

I approached slowly, cautiously. Being asked to go to a limo was not an everyday experience for me.

Chapter 8

I was two feet away from the long car when the door opened to reveal a cream leather interior and a familiar face. Madame Tinselle, designer dressmaker sat inside.

"Well," she said in a thick French accent, "get in."

I looked around again, still on edge from the feeling of being watched, before climbing into the spacious interior. Madame Tinselle curled a lip at the shopping bags I was carrying. I placed them on the floor and tried to hide them behind my calves so she couldn't see them. I regretted letting Mum take me shopping more than ever.

Madame herself was wearing an elegant gown made from a light plaid fabric of criss-crossing purples. Intricate pleats gave it a look that was both old-fashioned and modern. Not exactly my taste but it looked expensive.

One of the colours was the exact shade of pale lilac as her delicate gloves. The designer held out a hand to her assistant, who was sitting on the other side of the leather bench with a pinched expression on her face. Her assistant produced a newspaper so crisply folded it could have been ironed. She handed it to Madame Tinselle. The designer waved it at me without opening the paper.

"Is eet true?"

"Er…"

"Ze engagement. Are you going to be married to ze prince?"

"Er, yes."

"Bien. Congratulations. Zat ees good. Now, your wedding dress…" she looked at me expectantly with bright hazel eyes.

"Er, I haven't thought about a dress or anything. We only got engaged a week ago!" I was starting to get annoyed with all this interest in my wedding.

"Of course you have not thought of it. And you do not need to!" Madame Tinselle crossed her feet elegantly at the ankles to punctuate her point. She sounded triumphant, but I had no idea what she was talking about. I stared at her tiny shoes with stiletto heels and what looked like a wolf's head made of diamantes attached to the side.

"Er…"

The French woman let out a small sigh of irritation before explaining slowly, "You do not need to think of it because I will create a dress for you!" Her eyes became even brighter as she continued, "Eet will be such a dress as I have never before made. You will leave everything to me."

"Er…that's very, er, generous of you," Madame smiled beatifically at me, "but I was thinking of something a little simpler." The designer scoffed at that. I carried on, "I mean, you're the best there is and I would never be able to afford your…creation."

"Money! Always you dwarves think of money! But you will not worry. Eet is a gift."

"A gift?"

"Yes. Zat is what I said. Eet is a gift. From me to you. Hein, it is done."

The assistant pursed her perfectly shaped lips even more. I shook my head. "I can't possibly accept your offer. It's too much."

"No one turns down Madame Tinselle!" The assistant glared at me now with fire in her baby blue eyes. Her severe bun made her look even more fearsome.

Madame Tinselle turned her own stare on her assistant then placed her gloved hand over mine. Her beady eyes locked onto mine as she patted my hand, "Now, you zink I am doing zis for ze love of you. Non! Let me explain. You are a businesswoman, I know. Your wedding ees getting much attention. I will not allow you to wear anyone else. You will walk down ze aisle wearing my dress and when you are asked who you are wearing, you will say 'Tinselle'!"

Now I understood. I nodded weakly. The diminutive designer was a force of nature. "I don't have dates or a venue yet…"

She interrupted me, "Eet is no matter. Now let me look at you." She studied me appraisingly, "I zink you have not gained any weight since last year, non?" I tried to splutter something about my exercise regime. Madame held up a gloved hand to silence me. "I will contact you when eet is ready. Au revoir."

With that, the assistant tapped on the glass screen behind me for the driver to stop. I readied myself to get out, picking up the paper shopping bags containing new outfits for my trip to the dwarven city of Jarnstradr.

The limousine lurched forward.

I was flung from my seat onto the floor at Madame Tinselle's feet. The hard diamanté wolf on her shoe cut my lip. I felt the hot trickle of blood run down my chin. A drop of blood fell onto the fabric of her shoe, leaving a small red stain. I pushed myself back onto the seat.

"What are you playing at?" Madam Tinselle shouted at the driver. It was only later that I realised that her French accent had disappeared. Her assistant alternated between frantically pressing the button that lowered the glass and banging on the divider itself. A horn blared outside. I glanced out of the blackened glass window.

The limo swerved wildly across lanes of traffic. A city bus screeched to a halt. It was a miracle we hadn't hit anyone. I used the seatbelt to lever myself up and hammered my fist on the glass. Nothing. The sickening thought that the driver might have fainted crossed my mind. I gripped Bane, my double-headed ancestral axe, and pulled it from its holster. I yelled at Madame and her assistant to duck. Their eyes widened at my weapon and they sunk into the footwell. I swung the axe around as hard as I could. The glass shattered upon impact. Shards flew into the driver's compartment. Some crunched onto the leather seat next to me.

I felt the tang of compulsion on the driver. It was a twisted combination of hot metal and blood that set my teeth on edge.

The driver stared vacantly ahead. I followed his gaze. The limo careened off the road and onto a grass verge. We were headed straight for a building. I dropped my axe onto the plush seat, dived for the steering wheel and fought for control. My front half was in the driver's compartment while my feet flailed wildly in the passenger section. I tried to steer us back to the road. The driver was tall and strong. I barely caused the limo to judder from its path. He wasn't interested in fighting me. Instead, he focused on keeping the long vehicle on course.

Without thinking, I turned, grabbed Bane and brought the flat of my axe-head down on the driver's head, just below his traditional grey peaked cap. His head fell forward onto his chest and his arms went limp. The compulsion lifted once he was unconscious, and I lost the metallic sense I had experienced before. I dropped the axe and grabbed for the wheel again. I hit the indicators and several buttons in my wild dive. The radio switched from classical to punk rock. I pulled the steering wheel sharply to the right. Barely in time. The left side of the limousine scraped along the brick wall with a squeal that made me flinch. We bumped along the grass and back towards the road. I risked taking one hand from the wheel and reached over the unconscious driver, struggling to find the keys to switch the engine off.

"Press the button!" screamed Madame Tinselle's assistant from the back seat.

I looked down and saw the ignition button. I jabbed at it with one hand and furiously tried to steer the limo with the other. The engine cut out. Cars beeped as I steered us back into the road and away from pedestrians, some of whom I noticed filming the runaway limo with their smartphones. After a few hundred feet, the car had slowed to a crawl, and it came to a halt in a bus stop just past a hotel. I pressed the red triangular switch to activate the hazard lights and pushed myself back into the passenger area.

Chapter 9

Madame Tinselle patted her hair. It still looked perfect. The pleats in her purple plaid dress were a little crumpled though.

"You saved my life. How can I repay you?" the designer looked at me with her clear hazel eyes.

"Don't even worry about it," I muttered. She was already making me a wedding dress; I didn't want her to feel indebted to me. Instead, I scrabbled to find my shopping bags. I wanted to get home. Too late.

Approaching sirens heralded incoming police cars. Three white cars with flashing blue lights pulled up and redirected the traffic around us. I tried to slink away.

"Stop right there miss, we'll need to get a statement."

I sighed and turned back. I started to tell the police officer what had happened, but it was clear that he didn't believe my instincts that there had been some sort of compulsion on the driver.

"We'll have to take him down the station and run some tests, after he's had medical attention of course," he speared me with a look that clearly said that it was my fault he was unconscious.

I shifted uncomfortably. I mean, it was technically my fault, but I had stopped us from being killed, so that had to count for something.

An officer ambled over from where she had been taking statements from a number of drivers who had stopped to shout at the erratic limousine. She looked over her colleague's shoulder at his notepad.

"Haernson? As in Amethyst Haernson?"

I nodded and swallowed, wondering if this was about the time I'd had my axe confiscated by the police. Subconsciously, I gripped the handle where I'd rested it against my leg.

"The dwarf getting married to a prince? Wow! My Mum's not going to believe this. Sorry, this is unprofessional, but do you mind if I get a picture?" she pulled out her phone. Her colleague looked a lot more interested too now that he knew he was talking to someone who had been in the paper.

"Er…" I blinked and tried to smile as she took a selfie, the first officer insisting on getting in the picture too.

"Thanks, that's great!"

They exchanged broad smiles and looked around guiltily before the policewoman slipped her phone back into her pocket. She bounced on the balls of her feet excitedly.

The policeman coughed and eyed my axe. Good for photo props but apparently not so welcome in the city. It was enchanted so it was invisible from about six feet away.

Unfortunately, both police officers were close enough that the enchantment didn't work. He started asking me uncomfortable questions when Madame Tinselle swept up.

"Pish! Eet is clearly a cultural trinket zat dwarves wear. Ze height of fashion, I am sure. Now, are we finished? I am already late for my consultation with Cirian - perhaps you know him? He ees a singer…and my driver needs ze hospital! How am I to get to there?" I'm sure she gave me a wink as she linked her arm with the officer's and propelled him towards his squad car.

I crept away and got the bus home, clutching my axe and my paper bags full of new clothes that were now crumpled.

Chapter 10

I checked I had everything for the umpteenth time. The day of our departure had arrived quickly and now we were waiting for the car, and I was more anxious than ever.

My breath came out in clouds of mist in the early morning chill, cold for September. At least it wasn't raining. Puddles still lined the street from last night's downpour and glinted in pastel pinks and oranges in the dawn light. They looked like they might be portals to another world. I kicked one and watched the reflections of the apartment blocks ripple across the surface.

Another world? We might as well be going off planet. It had seemed like a good idea at the time. I tried in vain to smooth down my frizzy reddish-brown hair. The closer we got to leaving, the more nervous I became. I patted down the pockets in my trusty red leather jacket.

Schiztz! Where was the dzraking invite? I checked again. Nothing. Schiztz, schiztz, schiztz. Lorandir saw me frantically checking my jacket and arched a perfect eyebrow at me questioningly.

"I've lost the dzraking invite!"

"Check your inside pocket, you said you wanted to keep it safe," his calm voice was reassuring. If he was bricking it, the elf's cool exterior didn't betray any nerves.

I opened my jacket and found the piece of parchment I was looking for. I breathed a sigh of relief. That was the third time I'd lost it today, and we'd only been up for an hour. I thought back to the chaos of the morning. I had carefully laid the parchment on my bedside table last night. When I woke up this morning, it was gone. I had spent a frantic ten minutes searching for it before checking under the bed, where it lay innocently. I replaced it on my table before having a quick breakfast. When I came back, it was gone again. This time, Errol had decided it was some sort of plaything. It had taken half a bucket of coal and a lot of swearing before he'd stopped toying with me and let me take it. I still had the claw marks on my arm from that bout of play fighting. My hand went to the small wyrm, drowsing around Lorandir's neck. He was a pain, but I loved him.

"Where the dzrak are they?" I was impatient and the waiting was grating on my nerves. I was already on edge. Unwelcome thoughts started to make their way to the forefront of my mind. Maybe the dwarves had changed their mind, and I was the only one who didn't know. Maybe Mum and Dad had decided to go on their own and I'd misunderstood their message and they weren't taking me with them.

To distract myself, I touched the parchment again to check it was there before finding my phone in another pocket and then stroking the reassuring weight of my axe-head. It was like I was doing some sort of religious genuflection.

I rested my backpack on the small suitcase and opened it. Several chocolate bars looked up at me temptingly; was it ever too early in the morning for chocolate? I resisted. For now. Instead, I rifled under the chocolate to check my change of clothes were there. They were. Nothing had moved since I'd packed and repacked last night. I zipped the bag back up and contemplated the suitcase. It was full of more clothes courtesy of the shopping trip with Mum. But had I packed enough underwear? I bent down to unzip the case. Lorandir stopped me.

"It will be fine."

"You don't know that," I grumbled. He handed me a travel mug full of strong coffee laced with chocolate. I perked up as I sipped the bitter drink. My hand went to my backpack again. Surely it was time for a midmorning snack by now…

"Remind me again why we have to be up at this ungodly hour? I don't even have to be up this early for work," Aloora's voice interrupted my quest for sugar. She blinked at me, her eyes still heavy from sleep. She brought her small suitcase to a halt next to mine and took a swig from her own travel mug.

"Dad wanted to be there in plenty of time," I muttered as I checked my phone. My parents were already ten minutes late.

Instead of answering me, Aloora filmed herself in the flattering morning light and uploaded the video to her social media channels. She was more popular than ever as her online persona Aloora Dragonquest, now that there were really dragons in the world. I frequently wondered how she had the time to run numerous social media accounts, write up her

PhD, and hold down her job at the Magical Liaison Office. Overachiever didn't even begin to cover it.

A familiar burgundy Land Rover pulled up and Mum opened the window. "Well what are you waiting for? Get in!"

After depositing our suitcases in the spacious boot, we climbed into the back seat and belted up. Mum started enthusing about the night they'd spent at Lorandir's apartment. Mum was thrilled by the views over the Bay and the luxury finish on the kitchen. Dad had jumped at the chance not to fork out on a pricey hotel room in Cardiff, although he confided in me later that the penthouse was "Too bloody high up for a dwarf."

"I'd forgotten your Mum was a morning person," Aloora whispered to me. She pointedly put on her headphones and an eye mask that I'd never seen before and leant her head against the window to try to get some more sleep.

That left Lorandir and me to answer Mum's questions about anything that came into her head. By the time we got out of the city's one-way system, my head was swimming.

"And you've got the invite, love?"

I patted my jacket pockets. My heart leapt. Schiztz, where was it?

"Inside pocket," Lorandir supplied. I smiled at him and produced the parchment with a flourish before tucking it back safely into my pocket.

"Thank dzrak for that! I didn't want to have to turn around."

"Language Dafydd! Well, shall we have some music then?" Mum cranked the radio up. She hooked it up to her music device and shuffled through seventies and eighties hits. The music reminded me of car journeys from my childhood and I smiled. I was surprised that Lorandir could sing along though.

When I gave him a puzzled look, he simply shrugged, "What? I liked them when they were popular the first time around, not as good as the Beatles, of course, but catchy."

I smiled, but it was forced. Sometimes I forgot how old my fiancé was. And unwelcome thoughts wormed their way into my head for the rest of the journey; could an elf who was already over a hundred years old ever be happy with a half-dwarf?

We pulled into a service station for food just before midday, interrupting my spiralling thoughts. I selected a limp sandwich from the lacklustre selection and started chewing. I don't know how a ham and tomato sandwich can go so wrong, but this was the worst I'd ever eaten. I forced down a bite of bread that tasted like it had been made of cardboard, soggy from the tomato juices. The meat had a strange tang to it too.

I threw my disappointing sandwich away and resigned myself to snacking on chocolate in the car. Maybe I could stock up on road sweets while we were here.

Aloora picked at a salad and drank a homemade smoothie she had brought along. Mum produced hot pasties from her oversized bag and handed them out. They were a lot nicer than the sandwich. Back at the car, Aloora offered to drive. I saw Dad's eye twitch, but he didn't want to be rude.

"Best not, hey. After all, you're not insured."

"It's not a problem. My job's got cover for all sorts of vehicles."

"You're not on the clock now though, are you?"

Aloora met Dad's eyes with a smile, "I might be. Anyway, you'd be doing me a favour, I love driving."

"Go on, Dafydd, let her drive. You can get your head down for a couple of hours."

Dad knew he had lost as soon as Mum weighed in on Aloora's side. He climbed into the passenger seat and strapped himself in. Aloora sorted out the sat nav on her phone and started off. The wheel spin as we left the service station was not a good start.

"What's that?"

"Sat nav."

"You don't need sat nav when you've got me. I know the way like the back of my hand."

"What if there are road works?"

"That's when you use a map!" To my horror, Dad started unfolding a huge paper map from the glove box. "When I was younger, if you wanted to go somewhere, you had to use your own intuition."

"Dad, when you were younger, they didn't have cars!"

"Nonsense, us dwarves invented steam power long before humans. You'll still see the steam trucks in operation when we get to Jarnstradr!"

"I thought Watt invented the steam engine?"

"Where do you think he got the idea from? Now I'll tell you something interesting young elf…"

I turned my attention to the scenery flashing by while Dad droned on about some intricate valve system. It was rich calling Lorandir young. I tried to do some muzzy mental arithmetic and then stopped. I did not want to think that Dad might be only a few years older than my fiancé. That was too weird. I reassured myself that they looked nothing alike and decided I needed comfort food. I popped one of the jelly sweets I'd bought at the services into my mouth and grimaced.

I thought I'd bought regular jelly babies but as I studied the packet, I realised they'd changed all the flavours and made a special 'Summer Mix' pack. Ugh. I offered them round. No one wanted any. As we turned a corner, my head swam, and my stomach clenched.

"Pull over," I tried. No one heard me. "Pull over!"

Aloora took me literally and screeched the Land Rover to a halt. I stumbled over Lorandir and collapsed onto the grassy verge. Then I was violently sick.

Dzraking service station sandwiches. Dzraking 'Summer Mix' sweets. Prepared as ever, Mum offered me wet wipes, water and mints for my breath. It took the acid sting from the back of my throat.

"Ready to carry on?" Mum asked as she rubbed my back and held my hair out of my face. I nodded weakly and got back in the car. I managed to get some sleep for the rest of the way, snuggled against Lorandir's shoulder. Errol had vacated his usual spot and was snoring in the elf's lap.

I awoke as the car slowed. The sun was setting. We had been travelling for almost the entire day. Aloora steered the car towards a slow-moving line of vehicles heading for the side of a mountain. We had arrived.

Chapter 11

As we approached the mountain, I saw that the enormous metal doors were stood wide open to welcome visitors. I gulped. Stupidly, I had thought this would be a small ceremony. The number of cars in the winding queue showed me I was wrong. The setting sun turned the doors a reddish gold colour. It reminded me of a forge.

Dad sighed happily. This had been his home until he had met Mum on one of his trips outside the mine. Now he only went back to teach his metalworking skills to younger generations. He looked over at Aloora.

I'd misjudged him. The sigh of happiness was because Aloora had to keep the car at a snail's pace in the queue. The gnome tapped her fingers impatiently on the steering wheel.

A dwarf in a suit, with an electronic tablet in one hand, stopped us just before the huge doors. He stared at Aloora and then at Dad. Before Dad could say anything, Aloora reeled off a greeting in fluent Dwarfish and provided our names. I smiled at Dad's face and turned it into a cough behind my hand as he turned to glare at me. The guard asked for my invitation.

I frantically patted down my pockets again until Lorandir reminded me it was still inside my jacket. My face heated at the impassive look on the dwarf's face. I handed the invitation over. The dwarf took it, scanned something into his tablet, and handed it back. I could see gears whirring under the see-through case as the dwarf tapped in the number of guests.

He held the tablet up to the car and explained that he needed to scan us in and asked us to open all the windows. I hastily tried to flatten my hair for the scan. The dwarf paused when he saw Lorandir's face.

A slight twitch of his lips and a reddening of his cheeks was all that betrayed his fury at an elf being invited to the largest dwarven city in the UK. He scanned the elf's face and then waved us in. I heard him talking angrily into a phone as we drove off. I really hoped Lorandir couldn't understand Dwarfish, because I had no doubt he could hear every word.

My fiancé gazed around unconcerned as we drove into the city limits. I looked up at the gigantic metal doors as we crossed the threshold. Dwarfish runes for protection, luck, happiness, and many more were etched into the metal. I didn't need my enchanting goggles to know that they were imbued with magic.

There was a huge beam above us that doubled as a door frame and hid the huge gears and weights that allowed the doors to open and close seamlessly. We followed the directions of dwarves in high-vis vests taking us into a huge cavern.

Another dwarf in a neon jacket motioned us into a parking spot next to a Jeep. Dwarves clearly preferred utility vehicles.

Aloora cut the engine and we got out. The cavern was huge, lit by large spotlights hung up on the rocky ceiling. It had to be at least as large as the Millennium Stadium, if not bigger.

"Well, thank you for driving Aloora," Mum was polite. Dad's face was still paler than his usual ruddy complexion. I guessed he wouldn't let her drive again.

Another dwarf in a suit appeared with a trolley fashioned from wood with metal banding. He motioned for us to load in our suitcases. While we unpacked the car, he spoke into his sleeve and nodded.

I didn't catch every word, but he definitely said something about an elf. I glanced at Lorandir. His composure hadn't changed but I noticed his ears had gone slightly pink. So, he did speak some Dwarfish then. The dwarf moved his hands over the cart, and I felt the hum of magic.

"If you would follow me," he spoke in perfect English before setting off towards an opening in the cave at the other end of the carpark. The trolley followed obediently behind.

Mum and Dad linked arms and fell into line behind the suitcases. I held my arm out to Lorandir. He linked his arm through mine with a grateful smile at me, and we walked behind. As other dwarves took in our procession, I heard the mutterings start.

Hostile faces turned in our direction as we passed through the carpark and into a long tunnel. I kept my gaze straight ahead, my cheeks flaming. This was a bad idea. The tunnel opened abruptly into a huge cavern. The lighting here was more traditional, with magic torches spewing out smokeless flames. As well as the torches set into the rock, cast iron lampposts marked out the formal pathways through the cavern.

As we approached a circle of lampposts that ringed an indoor equivalent of a park, a dwarf stepped out to block our path.

Chapter 12

He was almost as broad as he was tall, and he planted his hobnail boots in a stance that suggested he wasn't moving. He crossed his hairy arms across his leather vest and stared hard at our group.

Our escort spoke to this dwarf in an angry tone with gestures towards the path and the park beyond. I stared over the dwarf's head at the indoor garden created from ferns, mosses, and interesting rocks. A fountain bubbled up from one of the larger boulders and cascaded down the stone in a pleasing babble. Above the public garden was an opening that showed the dark, orangey-blue of the twilight sky. I dragged my attention back to the argument. Things were getting heated. I glanced around. And we had an audience.

Many other dwarves had stopped and were staring at us. Arms crossed, eyes hard as they looked on. The hardest stares came from dwarves with long white beards pulled into styles that were fashionable maybe seventy years ago. Schiztz. They were silent for now, but I could feel the tension building.

The enclosed space intensified the mood. Dad joined in the argument and voices rose. My face turned bright red as I concentrated on the pure Dwarfish being flung around.

"I should have known you'd be involved Dafydd; you're a disgrace!"

"What's that supposed to mean?"

"It's bad enough you bring a human in here, but an elf! That's too far!"

A couple of shouts in the growing crowd supported the fat dwarf in front of us. I hoped Lorandir couldn't understand the insults being thrown his way.

Fatty stepped forward. His face was only a couple of inches away from Dad's. I stepped up to break up the fight before it started.

"What is going on here?" A short dwarf with a neat beard approached the shouting match with an air of authority.

The antagonist's eyes flashed but he stepped back and dipped his head to the newcomer. I recognised Master Ironfist now, his small face furious and his body vibrating with indignation.

"Dafydd Haernson is polluting our city with his human wife, half-breed daughter and pointy-eared elf."

"His daughter is here as the saviour of Avalon. She is being presented with the medal of honour, something that I believe no one in your family has ever achieved, Clodhammer. Prince Lorandir is here at her behest and as a personal friend to me, the first dwarven ambassador to the elves in five hundred years. I ask again, what is going on here?"

Clodhammer tried to outstare the small dwarf before he broke eye contact and looked away, "Nothing, nothing."

"Then I suggest you move, so our guests can proceed."

"Yes Master Ironfist," the dwarf stepped to one side and glared as we passed by.

I kept my eyes down for the rest of our procession. Ironfist led us himself to our quarters. On the way, he distracted everyone by sharing some of the city's history. I tuned out, second guessing my decision to bring my fiancé to the dwarf city. Then I got angry. Why couldn't I bring the love of my life to my cultural heartland? Lorandir looked at me questioningly and I forced myself to relax. The last thing I needed was him feeling more uncomfortable here but maybe it was fate that a dwarf and an elf could never be together, after all prejudices ran high between the two supernatural races.

I was pleased to see we were being housed in guest quarters away from the main open spaces. Dad had mooted the idea of us staying in the family mine with my grandmother. I had pointed out that Lorandir wouldn't be able to stand upright in the dwarf-sized mine and, more importantly, Gran had nearly fainted when I told her about our engagement. There was enough tension here, I didn't want to make Lorandir feel worse by forcing him to stay with my family.

Instead, Ironfist showed us to a series of high-ceilinged interconnected caves decorated with old oil paintings sitting alongside more modern metalwork. There was a pair of aged leather sofas and a smokeless fire flickering in an enormous fireplace that took up an entire wall. The heat would have made the room unbearable if it wasn't for the cunningly placed air vents that provided a cool breeze.

"Allow me to apologise for Clodhammer's unenlightened behaviour."

"It's not your fault. Clodhammer was always an idiot," Dad replied easily.

"Nevertheless, for your comfort, I will ensure you are accompanied while you are our guest here."

I looked at Ironfist, reading between the lines. We were going to have armed guards escorting us everywhere. This was turning into a nightmare.

"The kitchen is stocked, although it would be an honour if you would dine with me tonight."

Dad nodded along but I couldn't face a formal dinner. I rubbed my stomach, "I think I'll give it a miss. I've got a dickey tummy."

"I am sorry to hear that. Would you like me to fetch a surgeon?"

"No, no, I'm fine. I just want to rest."

"Of course," Ironfist executed a small bow and arranged a time for the others to visit his quarters. Lorandir gamely volunteered to stay with me. He looked composed on the outside, but the way he brushed his hair from his forehead told me the hostility he'd seen today had flustered him.

Chapter 13

I wheeled my suitcase along the perfectly flat rock floor to one of the bedrooms further in the cavernous suite. Dwarves had placed small crystals in the wall and enchanted to provide light. Lorandir touched one curiously.

"It's beautiful."

I studied the blue-green stone placed roughly at my eye line. "Apatite. It's meant to aid communication."

We carried on and I outlined all the properties of the gemstones that were lighting our way. There was pale green aquamarine to clear confusion and soothe fears. Polished black onyx and dark green jade to encourage wise decisions. Swirling green chrysoprase; another stone that helped with communication and truth. More gems lined the wall of our bedroom. As well as providing a soft, flattering light source, here the stones were arranged into patterns of dwarven artwork. Clusters of stones burst in representations of moons and constellations. I had never stayed in one of the Council's guest suites before. It was breathtakingly beautiful.

I recognised glowing pearls for integrity and honesty in one constellation on the ceiling. I blushed as another meaning whispered in my mind; fertility. Amidst the soft whites and polished greens, my fingers sought out my namesake stone in a swirling galaxy on the carved wall. Amethyst for protection, patience, creativity and balance. Not for the first time I wished I embodied those qualities. Lorandir stepped up behind me.

"Amethyst is my favourite jewel."

I turned and embraced him. Aloora bounded in.

"Oops, sorry. At least you're wearing clothes this time!"

I glared at her, "Don't you know how to knock? And we *were* wearing clothes last time you burst in on us…" I thought back to the time she had come home unexpectedly early from a library visit and caught us canoodling on the sofa in our flat.

"A cape isn't clothes." I blushed but my friend ignored me and carried on, "Have you seen the decoration here? I bet it hasn't changed in a millennium. I'll have to tell Shesalva; she's studying ancient art. Can I take a quick video?" Her phone was already in her hand. She stood in the middle of the room filming then tried to post it on her social media channels, "Dammit. No signal. How do dwarves stay connected down here?"

"You'll have to find their network, but I don't know if your phone will connect. Theirs are all powered by magic."

Aloora gave a snort of annoyance, "I can't be incommunicado while we're down here! I wish Maxi were here; he'd be able to hook me up."

I nodded along while ushering her out of the room. "Why don't you ask Ironfist at dinner? Shouldn't you be getting along?"

She returned to the communal living room, still stabbing at her phone with her forefinger. I closed the door purposefully as I heard my parents bustle down the corridor on their way out to meet the Council member. I put my hand on the nearest gemstone and willed my power into the rocks, commanding the lights to dim. Nothing happened.

I wasn't surprised. My affinity was for metal rather than stone. I searched for a switch and found a series of stones set into a metal panel. One was a red carnelian…a lustful stone. I cocked my head, making sure everyone else had gone before I pressed it and the glow from the gems in the wall dimmed to a moody setting.

"Now where were we?"

"Are you sure you're feeling up for this? You were pretty sick earlier…"

I kissed the elf passionately on the lips and pushed him to the king-sized bed as an answer. We made love by the light of hundreds of twinkling jewels. It was magical. As I dozed in the afterglow of great sex, I heard Lorandir mumble.

"How do you turn off the lights?"

I pointed to another series of gems set into a bronze panel near the bed and closed my eyes again. Lorandir pressed the stone furthest from the bed. Behind my closed eyes, bright light flared. I swore and covered my face with my arm. The elf cursed softly and selected another jewel.

The lights in the constellations flared one by one in an impressive lightshow. I sleepily wondered how the enchantments had been done. Lorandir swore again, muttering something about dwarves over complicating things.

He managed to select the carnelian again, and the stones dimmed to an atmospheric glow.

Finally, he found the right jewel and the lights went out with the exception of tiny rows of small crystals that illuminated the lighting panels. I drifted off into a deep sleep until a scream reverberated through the vent system and woke me.

Chapter 14

I jumped out of bed, grabbed my axe and ran to the door. The cool breeze prickled my skin with goosebumps. I looked down. I was naked! Grabbing a silk guest robe from a hook mounted on the wall, I yanked open the door and stepped out. I looked both ways. Nothing.

I stepped out into the corridor and followed the glowing crystals to the other guest rooms. I paused outside the first door. Dad's snores were loud enough to send soft vibrations through the wooden door. I kept going. At the next door, I heard liquid. Images of blood running from Aloora's prone body flashed through my head. I shoved the door open with my shoulder. She wasn't in the bedroom.

I followed the noise to the bathroom. I felt rather than heard someone behind me. I turned quickly, spinning with my axe out. Lorandir dodged my blow with easy elven agility and rested his hand on my arm. He was wearing his own robe. Being fashioned for a dwarf, it was practically indecent on him. I gave him a look that said he needed to be more careful about sneaking up on people. He opened his mouth to reply. I pressed a finger to my lips.

We needed to be quiet. If someone had snuck past our armed escorts, then surprise might be our only advantage. Taking a deep breath, I hefted Bane with one hand and rested my free palm on the bronze door handle. I pulled it open and ran in with a shout.

Aloora screamed. My shout turned into a scream of surprise. My friend was in a huge bath carved from soothing white agate. She dived for a towel, sending water all over the cave floor.

"I'll, er, just wait outside," Lorandir's gaze was firmly on the ceiling as he backed out of the bathroom. His ears had flushed a bright red.

I handed my friend a towel and rested my large axe on the floor, keeping my eyes on her face.

"What the dzrak are you doing Ame?" she glared at me as she dried her face and removed her headphones.

"I heard a scream! Are you OK?"

"Apart from you nearly giving me a bloody heart attack, I'm fine!" A twinkle had formed in the petite gnome's eye, she wasn't annoyed at me, "There are easier ways to see me naked than running in with an axe you know." She kept going before I could bluster a reply. "I slipped getting into the bath and hit my thigh on the edge. It's made from solid rock and it bloody hurt."

I looked at her thigh. There was a purplish bruise blossoming on her skin.

"Schiztz. Do you want Lorandir to take a look at it?"

"No thanks, I just want to enjoy my bath then look at the book Ironfist leant me. It's thrilling really, there are some descriptions of dragon riders and their commands." Her eyes misted over. Since befriending a dragon at Avalon, she was spending as much time as she could up in the magical reserve of Breconia. I could tell she was dreaming of riding him again.

"OK, well, I'll leave you to it then," she waved me away, and I retreated to my room.

Lorandir was seated on the bed, his head in his hands, mortified. I patted him awkwardly on the shoulder. The robe was now doing even less to hide his body.

"Hey, if seeing an attractive gnome naked is the worst thing that happens today, then it'll be a good day." He looked at me, confused. "It's the day of the ceremony for that dzraking medal of honour. I wish I'd never accepted the stupid thing. It's not as if the dwarves want me here. I only accepted it to make Dad proud and look how that's working out. It started a dzraking argument in the middle of the city as soon as we arrived!"

"Your Dad is proud of you," he pulled me towards him. We held each other for a moment before I broke away with a sigh.

"Better get dressed I suppose."

"How about we check out our own bathroom first…"

Chapter 15

I was starving by the time we had bathed and made sure we were both thoroughly clean. I had taken my time selecting my outfit for the ceremony. The red dress I'd picked on the shopping trip with Mum flattered my figure, and, with the help of some supportive underwear, my curves looked firm and deliberate rather than the result of my sweet tooth.

I had traded in my gothic style heavy-duty leather boots for a pair of court heels on Mum's advice. They were uncomfortable, but they added a sway to my step and a couple of inches of height. I braided my hair into two plaits to keep the bushiness at bay. I had checked myself out in the polished onyx mirror in the bathroom. I looked pretty good.

Lorandir had foregone the traditional elven robes he'd brought with him and decided to blend in with a suit that he'd brought as a back-up outfit. He looked like a popstar with his tousled blonde hair and killer good looks.

Despite the pressure from my tight fat-busting pants, I was still hungry. We made our way to the kitchen. After some fumbling with the crystals that doubled as light switches, I found a setting that wasn't quite as bright as staring into the sun and set about looking for food.

Ironfist hadn't lied about the kitchen being well stocked. Someone had filled the cupboards with traditional dwarven fare. I pulled out some dried meat jerky and started cutting it up. Mum bustled in wearing a blue dress with a ruffle at the bottom of the skirt. She smiled at us and immediately took over, chopping and frying fresh mushrooms and buttering bread.

I grabbed a slice of toast to tide me over and glanced nervously at the large clock carved into the wall above the still-blazing fire. Three hours to go. Dad strolled in wearing a garish waistcoat made from soft, thin leather covered with neat chainmail links over a crisp shirt. Sweat stains had already started to appear through the linen shirt. The waistcoat had purple amethysts set into the chainmail. He'd paired it with a leather belt, leather trousers, and hobnail boots that were polished to a high shine. His hair and beard were slick with oil. He looked like he could have been in some sort of well-dressed motorcycle gang.

Aloora joined us just as we sat down to eat. She had chosen a fitted suit that made her look taller than she was and went well with her short pixie cut. She smiled at me as she removed her jacket to sit down. The golden dragon scale necklace I had gifted her last year sparkled under the crystal lighting. I smiled to see her wearing my best work.

"You scrub up well."

"So do you."

In hindsight, it probably wasn't the best idea to eat while wearing our best clothes. Dad got some spicy sauce in his beard and had to go and clean it out and then re-oil it. The leather was wipe-clean though, so he could easily clean off the blob of ketchup that fell onto his trousers. I huffed at his clumsiness then dropped a mushroom into my cleavage. Like father, like daughter.

I retrieved it quickly, but the mushroom had been cooked in rich butter. Mum gasped as she saw the dark stain spread. She ran for a wet wipe while I stood and tried to pat the grease away with a napkin. Schiztz. Of course, this would happen to me. Mum did the best she could while I finished up my sausage sandwich. No one saw the dollop of red sauce that fell onto my thigh.

I mopped it up with a new napkin surreptitiously and breathed a sigh of relief when I realised it was the exact colour of the dress. Lorandir and Aloora, of course, ate without making a complete mess.

I was still putting the finishing touches to my makeup when Lorandir interrupted me to inform me that our escort was here. Schiztz. I smudged the mascara trying to put it on too quickly and dabbed at my face with a tissue. That made it worse. I wetted my finger with my tongue and managed to get the smear of black goop off my face. I checked myself again in the flattering onyx mirror. I would do. Just one thing left.

Chapter 16

"What are you wearing?" Mum hissed. Dad nodded approvingly behind her.

"My axe," my hand went reflexively to the top of the double-headed axe hanging from a belt at my hip.

"It doesn't go with your outfit!"

"It's an axe, Mum. It goes with everything."

I breezed past her and led the way out of our quarters. I paused on the threshold and tried to channel the most confident person I knew; Agent Jones. With her in mind, I squared my shoulders and marched out.

Four armed guards were waiting for us, dressed in kilts and suit jackets. They had their own axes slung at their waists and I guessed there were more weapons hidden in the leather sporrans they sported. I caught sight of a knife strapped under a knee-high white sock threaded with black silk ribbons. These dwarves meant business.

The dwarf I assumed was in charge because of his larger axe, nodded and set off at a brisk pace. We followed behind in a tight group. Two dwarves took up places on either side of our small band, and one brought up the rear, so they surrounded us in a diamond formation. The flickering flame-effect torches and polished stones that bounced the torchlight around meant we could see clearly underground. In the daytime, I caught the thick scent of baking wafting through the large tunnel and the sounds of shopkeepers plying their wares.

"Oh Dafydd, we must go shopping while we're here. Look at those candelabras!"

"I could make you something like that."

"You say that, but you never do."

My parents' bickering fell away as we moved out of the main cavern and into a smaller tunnel. This tunnel was lined with glittering diamonds for purification and cleansing. I recognised it as one of the paths to the Dwarven High Council. Lorandir had to hunch over to fit through. I smiled at him nervously. I thought again that it might not have been the best idea to bring an elf to a dwarven city. Where we were trapped. Underground.

The tunnel opened abruptly into a large garden. Lorandir straightened with relief after the cramped passageway. Like the park in the main cavern, this one was lit by an opening to the sky. Rain fell softly through the carved hole and the plants gleamed in the magical light. More jewels placed among the plants provided calming energy and encourage openness. I wondered if that boded well or badly for the upcoming ceremony.

We stepped around the garden, avoiding the slippery surface created by the falling rain. The guards led us into one of several tunnels that opened off the garden. I heard Lorandir give a resigned sigh as he stooped again to fit through the tunnels carved so they were above average dwarf height but couldn't accommodate the lofty elf.

Partway along the tunnel, there was a metal door flung open so it rested against the smooth surface of the rock. The lead dwarf paused. Ironfist stepped forward. His white beard shone in the light of more diamonds studded into the walls.

"Amethyst! Welcome! If you would come this way…" He gestured into the room. I stepped towards him and then looked at the others. The lead dwarf had stepped between them and me. I swallowed, my hand reaching for my axe.

"Silver here will escort your guests to their places, you can wait here until you are called," the elderly dwarf beamed at us.

Mum stepped forward to give me a quick kiss on the cheek. Dad gripped my shoulder, "I'm proud of you love."

Aloora scooped me into a tight hug, "Good luck, you'll smash it!"

Lorandir's embrace was awkward in the cramped space, "I love you galad, Amethyst."

"I love you too," I whispered back. I heard one of the guard dwarves suck in a disapproving breath. My face heated with embarrassment. Another guard elbowed the first in the stomach. They led my family away. I leaned against the cool metal and felt alone.

Chapter 17

Ironfist offered me his arm and I took it. He led me along a narrow tunnel studded with more diamonds. They didn't skimp on the jewels for the Dwarven Arms Council.

"You probably don't want advice from an old dwarf, but you should not care about what they think."

"Huh?" I was articulate as ever.

"The dwarves. You are here to receive the highest honour of dwarfdom. They are jealous of your success. If you act like their approval matters to you, then they will disapprove all the more. Ignore them."

"So what am I supposed to do? Just ignore all the comments and stares? You heard what they were shouting at Dad yesterday and he's a master craftsdwarf. Why am I here Ironfist?"

He paused in front of a golden door that fitted perfectly against the tunnel opening. He patted my hand but had the grace to look mildly uncomfortable. "I put your name forward for the medal."

"What?!"

"I wanted you to get the honour you deserve. You have done more for dwarfdom in less than two years than the Council has in hundreds. It is time to shake things up and you can do it."

"You'll be nominating me for the dzraking Council next." Ironfist looked away uncomfortably. "Oh no, what have you done?"

"Now now, do not worry, it is not what you think," he reassured me, "we are simply debating the meaning of dwarfdom this afternoon. I would like you to be there."

That sounded like the opposite of what I wanted to do.

"And another thing, I have found something about your axe…" a horn echoed through the corridor, "but now is not the time. You must prepare." Ironfist murmured a word and the golden door opened effortlessly.

He ushered me inside and then left. I stared after him. What did he mean by prepare? No one had mentioned any tests. The door clanged shut behind me with a dull metallic thump. Schiztz. What was I supposed to do now? I looked around and took in four dwarves sitting on seats carved from rock. I felt four pairs of eyes stare intensely at me.

I took my own stone chair, arranging an animal skin over the rock so it was more pleasant to sit on. I glanced at the seated dwarves and regretted my dress. They had come in more traditional outfits. Leather. Chainmail.

One of them even had a polished steel breastplate strapped to their chest. It was all dress armour for sure, but it was armour. I hadn't even brought a jacket. I didn't know how they could stand it in the heat of the caves. I was too hot, and

I only had half-dwarf blood flowing through my veins. A bead of sweat dripped down my forehead. Would I have to fight for the medal?

A female dwarf stood and walked over to me. She planted herself in front of me, tilted her head on one side and looked me up and down.

"Can I help you?"

She blinked in surprise at my Dwarfish, "Just looking at the half-breed who's earned herself a medal of honour. Can you even use that axe?"

My natural instinct was to keep my head down but Ironfist's words sounded in my head, *'If you act like their approval matters to you, then they will disapprove all the more.'* So I met her hazel eyes levelly, "Can you?"

Her fingers reached for her own pickaxe. She stopped as a booming laugh rolled around the room. We both turned towards a large dwarf slapping his thighs. "She got you there, Dirtbiter!" He stood and strode over to us. He held out his hand to me, "Well met Ms Haernson. I am Euan of the Stoneforge clan."

I stood and gripped his forearm in a traditional dwarven greeting, "Well met Euan and please, call me Amethyst or Ame."

He clapped me on the shoulder, "It is a great honour to be alongside the slayer of Mordred on this day. You have already met Dirtbiter. Allow me to present Bryn Tunneldriver and Paloma Rockaxe."

Bryn nodded at me, and Paloma put her hand over her heart and gave me a small, seated bow.

"I, er, didn't exactly slay Mordred."

The silence rang loudly.

"I knew it. You're a fraud!" Dirtbiter stepped forward, fists raised.

"She must have done something to be nominated," Euan looked at me with pleading eyes.

"Er, well I did fight him to protect the centre of Avalon's power…"

"There, you see, she laid her life on the line to protect Avalon. A mere half-dwarf going up against a powerful sorcerer," Euan beamed at me.

"And, er, are you all here to get the medal as well?"

"Bryn and Paloma slew a minotaur in the battle of Avalon and Dirtbiter…"

"I can tell my own story. It's not as impressive as not killing Mordred," her voice dripped with sarcasm, "but I distracted a group of dark elves so the injured could escape. I just did what any dwarf would do."

"Distracted a group of dark elves!" Euan snorted, "So modest. You placed yourself in danger for your comrades, fought ten of the evil creatures single-handedly and pulled several of our brethren to safety!"

"And why were you nominated, Euan?" I interrupted as Dirtbiter clenched her fists again.

"Me? Why I fought a great battle with a troll. Tales will be told of our battle through the ages. He brought down a club twice the size of me. I leapt to one side and cleaved his hand from his body. Undeterred, he picked up his club with his other hand and swung at me. Once! Twice! Thrice!" Euan punctuated his account with thrusts, acting out his triumph, "I used my hammer, the great Bonecrusher, to bloody his knees. The beast fell to the floor. From there I had him…" Another horn blast ricocheted around the room. "But enough of my glory, it is time to go!"

The dwarves led the way through another crystal studded corridor. It opened out into a huge cave. The Hall of the Dwarven Arms Council.

Chapter 18

I followed the band of dwarves as they marched to a spot on the right of the opening. We stood in a row. There was a smattering of applause, followed by silence. I looked around surreptitiously. I took in the carved stone benches with intricate Celtic style knots etched into the ends.

The members of the Council sat behind a long stone table. Five huge scrolls balanced on the rightmost end. Rows of stone benches stretched up into the cave in a large semi-circle facing the table. There were several dark caverns that I recognised as more entrances to the Hall. I turned my head and saw my guests seated on the front row of a carved stand.

They weren't hard to spot as Lorandir was a good deal taller than the dwarves who craned their necks to see past him. I saw Uncle Owain and Dylan sat next to him, wearing big grins and waving. I grinned back.

I wasn't sure how they had wangled their way into the ceremony, but I was glad they had made the trip from their wyrm farm where they looked after the abandoned animals.

Aloora gave me a thumbs up and, to my horror, Mum took out her camera. I spotted a guard making a beeline for her and a quick, heated discussion rebounded around the room before she put the camera back into her bag with a huff. Dwarves looked down at her disapprovingly.

The seating for the onlookers reminded me of pictures I'd seen of the Colosseum. We stood on a floor made of polished onyx. I hoped we wouldn't have to fight each other for the Medal of Honour.

The oldest council member, with a beard that fell to the floor, stood. A hush fell over the Hall. The ceremony had begun. The council member told the story of the founding of the Medal of Honour, how it was the highest prize in dwarfdom and was created by Bloodhammer the first as a reward for his prized lieutenant Goldhand.

I forced myself to stay still. I started with my gaze on the floor. The council member continued on in archaic Dwarfish. I got the gist, but I couldn't follow it exactly. I looked at my family again. Aloora and Dad were listening raptly. Of course, they could understand every word.

Lorandir had a practised, attentive expression borne from his experience as a member of the elven royal family, but his eyes had glazed over. Mum gave me a small wave. I waved at her without taking my hand away from my hip. I turned my eyes to the ceiling.

Three immense glowing chandeliers of cut diamonds gave out a pure white light so bright that I forced my gaze back to the floor. The onyx dulled the reflection so I could study the chandeliers in more detail. The stones had been worked into pointed stars of every size. They reminded me of the toppers you can get for Christmas trees, only much more brilliant. The dwarf behind the table began listing all previous dwarves who had received the medal going back thousands of years.

I mentally recited in my head the meanings associated with diamonds while he droned on: courage, strength, purity and health. They also drive away negative energy. There was one more meaning…I wracked my brains. My eyes lit on Lorandir. Love. That was the other meaning. I felt my face soften into a slight smile and immediately forced myself to concentrate on the ceremony. I was not going to be one of those soppy fiancées who went all weak-kneed at the thought of marriage.

A new dwarf – a female with long oiled hair flowing freely – started reading from a scroll. Her chest rose and fell under her heavy-duty leather vest as her voice chanted. It was a list of names. From the way heads were bowed, I gathered these were dwarves who had fallen during the battle of Avalon and were receiving the medal posthumously. I bowed my head. So many lives lost.

The horror of my first and only battlefield experience still haunted my nightmares. It could so easily have been any of us dead. It didn't seem fair that Mordred had caused so much suffering. I heard a stifled sob from one of the front benches. A family grieving for their fallen son or daughter. A lump came to my throat. The names stopped abruptly, and an expectant silence filled the hall. The dwarves next to me straightened their spines. I followed suit.

The female dwarf called Euan forward. The hall erupted into applause and stamping boots. A cacophony of noise reverberated around the chamber. I watched as Euan strode solemnly across the smooth floor to the stone table. An elderly Councilmember handed him a large scroll sealed with black wax. He bowed his head and murmured something as the dwarf pinned a small lump of metal to his vest. His chest swelled with pride, and he flashed a smile at a group of dwarves standing on their feet and waving. He swaggered over to the far side of the table and stood there grinning as he held his scroll.

One by one the other dwarves' names were called, and the process was repeated. Paloma got a few cheers as well as the applause. She was popular. Then I stood on my own. The Councilmember looked across at me. My throat dried out. I swallowed hard. Had there been a mistake?

I knew I shouldn't be here. I wasn't even a full dwarf. I felt my cheeks heat up. Sweat caused my dress to cling uncomfortably to my back. I heard my name. I breathed a sigh of relief I hadn't known I was holding.

Slowly, carefully, I walked in my kitten heels across the onyx floor. The floor vibrated slightly as I moved over it. I kept my head down, concentrating on each step. The last thing I needed now was to fall over in front of everyone who was anyone in dwarven society.

It was only when I got to the table that I realised the room was quiet. My face heated. No applause for the half-dwarf. The Councilmember looked down at me from his raised platform behind the table. He handed me my scroll. I gripped it tightly, crushing it in my hand.

"Thank you for your service, Amethyst Haernson," his voice was clipped and formal. He bent forward, holding a medal in the shape of a traditional pickaxe. He reached towards my chest, thought better of himself and instead pinned the heavy medal to my shoulder. The gold stood out against my dark red dress.

I nodded and bowed my head. I heard a whoop and turned. Aloora jumped to her feet, cheering next to Mum, who had tears running down her face. Lorandir stood and clapped loudly. Dad bellowed his support at me. Uncle Owain and Dylan stamped their feet and whistled through their neat beards.

The applause rippled out around them, as if the audience was embarrassed not to have shown support. I smiled and stood up straighter. I gave a small wave, then strode over to join the other medal recipients. We beamed at each other. Even Dirtbiter gave me a nod of comradeship.

The first Councilmember stood again and motioned for quiet. He was five words into what was going to be a long, rambling closing speech when we heard the rumbling.

Chapter 19

The rumbling continued, growing louder until it echoed around the hall. The crowd looked from side to side to try to pinpoint the noise. Not part of the traditional ceremony then. Undeterred, the Councilmember raised his voice until he was shouting about glory and bravery. The chandeliers swayed from side to side, their light casting long shadows as they moved. It wasn't my imagination; the floor was definitely shaking.

I looked at my fellow medal holders. They were all resting their hands on their weapons. I did the same, easing Bane out of my belt until I could fit my entire hand below the blade. The vibrating floor sent the elderly Councilmember lurching sideways. Finally, he stopped talking. I caught the glint of fear in his eyes. He shouted something to his fellow Councilmembers. They looked at each other nervously just before a hideous head burst through the wall behind them.

Someone screamed. A wave of familiar and uncomfortable magic stuck in my throat. That same coppery tang that reminded me of corruption and the taint of death. The amethyst pendant at my neck heated as its protective magic responded to the threat and flowed through me. I reached to my head for my enchanting goggles. Schiztz. I'd left them in the suitcase.

"A dzraking goliath!"

"Biggest dzraker I've ever seen!" Dirtbiter's voice pulled me back to the present.

The Dwarven Arms Council disbanded quickly. A couple hid under the huge stone table. Others ran for the doors. One Councilmember stood staring at the huge grey creature that writhed its way into the cavern. His eyes wide with surprise or shock, he didn't move as the hideous monster bore down on him.

Euan moved first. He ran and knocked the grey-bearded dwarf to the side. Without stopping, he turned and threw his hammer at the beast's stumpy snout. It connected with a meaty thump before bouncing to the floor. The huge worm-like creature let out a bellow of rage that sent blue flecks of saliva across the room.

I turned, ready to flee. I took in the horde of dwarves crowding around the tunnels that led away from the chamber. They pushed and shouted, shoving to get out of the chamber. Aloora stood in the centre, calmly directing the crowd, as if she did this sort of thing all the time. Mum stood next to her. Was that a camera in her hands?

I turned away as someone shouted my name. Lorandir moved against the crowd, coming towards me. I couldn't see Dad. I looked around me. The three other medal recipients had joined Euan to fight the beast. Schiztz. I tapped the gold medal on my shoulder. I had just received the Medal of

Honour. The highest honour in dwarfdom. And I was thinking about running away. I clenched my teeth. Drawing Bane, I entered the fray with a yell.

My blade bit into the greyish white skin and blue blood oozed from the wound. Angered, it turned its ugly face to me. I reeled back from its mildewy breath and rows upon rows of pointed teeth. It lunged at me. I leapt to one side as it slithered forward. My heel caught in between two of its sharp fangs. I flexed my foot and abandoned my shoe. Panting, I slipped the other kitten heel from my foot and ran. Once I was far enough away to make out its four bulbous black eyes on the top of its head, I threw the shoe with all my might. I watched the dainty heel spin over and over as it flew through the air. A roar told me I had connected with one of its eyes.

"Nice aim," Lorandir was by my side. I smiled at him. "What's this thing doing here? I thought they hated noise and light."

"They do…normally," I thought back to the tang of tainted magic, "it's being compelled!"

The elf let off a bolt of magic at the same time as the goliath slid left. The magic went wide and hit the cave wall, causing a small landslide.

"Bloody elf magic!" I heard someone shout. Lorandir's ears turned pink in embarrassment, and I felt his power as he gathered another bolt. I put a restraining hand on his arm.

"Don't. If you cause a cave-in, I'll never hear the end of it!"

He shook his hand to relieve the build-up of magic and sighed with frustration. I ran back to the dwarves fighting the creature. They ranged in a large semi-circle, taking turns to run in and hit it. It twisted its colossal head and snapped with angry jaws. It got a dwarf by the leg and clamped hard. The sharp teeth, each bigger than my forearm, sliced through his flesh like it was nothing. The dwarf cried out, then twisted and aimed its war hammer at the goliath, taking out pounds of flesh as it bit through his leg.

"Take that you dzraker!" I recognised Euan's voice, shaking with pain. The others tried to distract the beast with more blows.

"Aim for the eyes!" I yelled. I was in the fray now. I grabbed the trapped dwarf under the arm and braced myself. Lorandir's hands laced around my waist, lending me his aid. The creature was too strong. It dragged us with it as it turned to face more blows. I leaned back, trying to keep my feet. A blow landed somewhere to my left. The goliath roared. We took the opportunity and pulled. Euan came free. His leg was gone beneath the knee. Lorandir and I dragged him as far from the writhing creature as I could. He tried to push himself up.

"You fought bravely, but you're done."

"Nonsense! It's just a flesh wound! I've got another leg!"

"Your adrenaline is high and you're going to go into shock. Let me treat you." Euan gave Lorandir a look of mistrust combined with fear. "I promise, I can help you."

I gripped Euan's forearm tightly, "You can trust him."

The injured dwarf looked from me to the elf, then nodded and Lorandir poured his golden healing magic into Euan's body. The dwarf's breathing eased. I mouthed a silent thank you to my fiancé and headed back into the battle. Lorandir looked on with concern. He had left his sword in Cardiff to avoid antagonising the dwarves. A decision I was sure he regretted.

Chapter 20

The dwarves cleaved chunks of flesh from the huge grey-white worm. It thrashed in anger and fought its way further into the hall. Bluish-grey blood leaked from its damaged body. The kilted guards joined the battle. One threw a blade at the goliath's round eye. The black sphere popped and oozed down the creature's face. The knife's hilt glinted under the swaying diamond lights. I ran towards the creature.

I slipped on a puddle of frothy saliva and skidded across the polished onyx floor. Using the momentum, I brought my axe round and slammed into its side. The blade bit deep and I held onto the handle as the monster whipped itself round. I willed the blade to loosen, swearing at it and pulling as the goliath shook me from side to side. I felt magic flow through the axe, and it slipped free. I gave a shout of triumph and jumped clear of its writhing body.

I recognised Ironfist's neat beard as he approached the creature from the side and stepped up to the rocky entrance the goliath had made. He placed his hands to the wall and willed the worm-made tunnel to constrict. The mountain began to respond, but the creature was furious. It moved with a strength I hadn't seen before, and its thrashing body loosened the new stones as soon as Ironfist rearranged them.

Incensed at being squeezed by its own tunnel, the creature lurched forward and crushed Paloma against the huge stone table with a sickening thud. The force of the creature's body cracked the long piece of marble into shards. The goliath shook its head at the sound. But the compulsion kept it coming. We couldn't drive it away. We would have to kill it. A hand clapped my shoulder. I let out a shriek and turned.

"Hold it there, Amethyst!"

"Dad! Wait, where's Mum?"

"She's safe with Aloora. I thought you could use some help," Dad brandished his dagger.

We clasped forearms and moved into the battle. Dirtbiter was using her daggers to climb the creature. She sank the blades in deeply and pulled herself up its flank. The goliath reared up and hit the carved ceiling. I heard an ominous crack and looked up. A chandelier fell. I pushed Dad to one side as the cut diamonds smashed into the polished floor where he had been standing.

I looked round. Dirtbiter slumped unconscious against a wall. Schiztz. Her daggers were still embedded in the goliath. The creature turned towards me. I knew what I had to do. I ran to one side.

Blinded by the dazzling light of the remaining chandeliers, the goliath tracked sound, not movement. My bare feet were silent as I made my way to the blades sunk into its side. I strapped Bane back into my belt and jumped.

I collided with the slimy side of the goliath, scrabbled against its thick hide and grabbed the leathered hilt of a dagger. Holding on tightly, I reached up for the second blade. I tried to swing myself around and up. It wasn't often I wished to be an elf, but right now I longed for Lorandir's agility.

My face pressed against the creature's clammy, muscular side. It was moist and smelled somehow of fish and mould. I tried not to gag. A thud sounded by my knee. I looked down.

A new dagger protruded from the goliath. I planted my foot onto its handle and pushed up. Another thud. This time above my head. I reached for it. I twisted my head over my shoulder. Dad was directing a small band of dwarves to help me climb. I smiled at him, then turned back to the moving creature. I held on tight as it reared up to attack someone I couldn't see. An axe sailed over my head, clipping my ear.

"Dzrak it all, watch where you're aiming!" Dad yelled over the din.

I heaved my weight onto the new handhold. I felt the blade shift in the monster's flesh. Schiztz, schiztz, schiztz. The axe came loose in my grip. I swung wildly away from the creature's flank, holding on by one dagger. The goliath convulsed. I tightened my hold on the dagger's hilt. Schiztz. This was how I was going to die. Flung from a monster worm in a cave of dwarves. Air whooshed past me.

I looked up. Another dagger. They were coming fast now, forming a row of hand and footholds up the creature's side. I stretched up. I felt the welcome touch of a sturdy hilt against my palm, and I continued my awkward climb. Then I was atop it.

I crawled along its back to its ginormous head. Under my bare knees, I felt its muscles bunch with every movement. I kept low. It lurched towards Dad and the guards. Dzrak it. I tried to hurry. There was a moment of calm as the creature decided who to attack first. I stood and ran. My bare feet pounded on its thick hide. I couldn't let it kill my father!

I tore Bane free from its holster as I went. Then I was behind its remaining eye. I took a wide stance. I silently thanked Espretha for our training sessions. I hefted my ancestral axe and swung. Hard. Bane glowed and sunk deep into the last eyeball. It exploded in a gooey mess of black and blue slime.

The goliath writhed under my blow and bellowed a guttural roar. I pulled my axe free and struck it again and again. The creature roared in pain until it was silent. In my hands, the axe and I seemed to move as one. The runes covering its blade glowed and urged me on. I continued to strike it until I felt Lorandir's cool hands around my own.

"It's dead, Amethyst. It's over."

I felt my pendant cool as the tainted magic ebbed away. I sank into the elf's arms, suddenly drained.

Chapter 21

I pushed myself up. "Dad!" I shouted as I surveyed the remains of the Hall of the Dwarven Arms Council from atop the corpse of the goliath. I couldn't see him. Tears welled up in my eyes. This was not how this was supposed to go.

"I'm here, love," his voice called up from the ground.

Thank dzrak. I patted Lorandir's hand, and we ran to the edge of the huge creature's body. I slid down the slimy flesh of the goliath and landed in a heap on the floor. I pushed myself up and into Dad's arms.

"I thought I'd lost you!"

"It'll take more than a goliath to kill Dafydd Haernson," he squeezed me tightly. Thunder sounded in my ears. I released him and looked around, prepared for another monster to attack.

It took me a minute to recognise the sound wasn't the rumble of a goliath but cheering and stamping feet. The dwarves were celebrating the death of the beast. No. They were cheering me. I gave a half smile and the cheers continued for a full minute.

The lights rocked as the remaining chandeliers swung slowly before coming to a halt. A hole gaped in the wall behind the goliath. The huge worm's corpse lay half in and half out of it, oozing blueish blood. The impressive marble table had shattered into thick irregular slabs. Thin cracks spread along the onyx floor where the diamond chandelier had fallen.

Dwarves groaned and limped throughout the cavern. I nodded to Lorandir and he sped off to offer his healing powers. Mistrustful at first, the injured dwarves soon softened when Euan hobbled over, using his giant Warhammer as a crutch and extolling the elf's praises. I rolled my eyes. They would be bosom buddies by the time we left. Dad limped over to where Ironfist was directing a group of dwarves wearing masks and holding machetes. I tried not to throw up as they started carving up the body.

"Ah, Amethyst, slayer of the mighty goliath! And Dafydd! Well done, and please accept my gratitude on behalf of all dwarves here today."

"My wife?"

"I believe Ms Dragonquest escorted her back to your rooms." Dad turned with a grunt and hobbled off.

I hesitated, "The goliath, I think it was compelled by something else…" I stopped. It sounded crazy.

"I see. I will make the necessary investigations."

I made to follow Dad, thinking of a hot shower and the soft, warm bed back in our quarters. Ironfist interrupted my daydream. "Amethyst, if I may, I have something to show you when you're cleaned up. Would you meet me at the Weapons Hall?"

"A bit late for weapons, isn't it?" I looked pointedly at the slain goliath.

Ironfist laughed, "It's about your axe…"

"What about my axe?"

"All in good time, all in good time. See you there in two hours."

I was about to protest that I could be ready sooner, but then I looked down at my stained dress and the goo over my legs from straddling the monster. A shower had never seemed more appealing. I set off in the direction of the nearest tunnel, then turned back.

"What about your debate on dwarfdom?"

"Do you really want to come to the debate?"

Ironfist waved me away. Something good had come out of the goliath attack if it meant I didn't have to listen to a long-winded Council discussion.

As I passed the dwarves cleaving the corpse, one of them threw a hunk of the meaty flesh onto a cart. Blue-green bodily fluids spattered my cheek. I hurried on.

Mum stopped her pacing and pulled me into a tight hug as soon as I got back to our quarters. I'd gotten lost and somehow turned away from the main street. A passing female dwarf had taken pity on me and escorted me back to the central park, where I got my bearings. I reassured Mum I was alright and left out the bit about me climbing on a goliath's back and killing it. Aloora gave me a look that said she would be after all the details later, but she let me go, wrinkling her upturned nose at the stench of the creature's gooey innards on my clothes.

The bath was as luxurious as I remembered it. I slathered myself in soap and the water turned grey as I sloughed the fluids off my skin. Once I was sure I was clean, I emptied the bath and refilled it. I was tempted by the walk-in steam room set into a corner of the huge bathroom but decided against it. Instead, I closed my eyes and relaxed.

When Lorandir arrived, I offered him the bath, but he declined, opting instead for a quick flannel wash. He had a smear of blue on his face, but that was it. His clothes weren't even stained. My new dress was ruined. I had stuffed it into the small copper bin by the sink. I knew from experience that goliath goo wasn't easy to get out.

Once my toes and fingers had wrinkled, I decided to get out. I mentioned to my fiancé that Ironfist wanted to meet at the Weapons Hall and he merely nodded and selected a pair of perfectly fitted jeans and a top to replace his tailored suit.

Back in the lounge, Ironfist was waiting for us. Apparently, he'd decided to escort us personally.

"…and so you see we were thinking about redesigning the Council's guest chambers and Dafydd's always mentioned your excellent taste and experience decluttering. I wondered if you would be so kind as to talk to Quartz here, our resident interior designer, and share your ideas for our guest quarters?"

Mum blushed deeply, "Of course, I'd love to! Those rocks are a bit on the nose don't you think?" Rupert swallowed hard at Mum's assessment of carefully planned crystals, "But I don't like to leave Dafydd and everyone bored…"

"Ah, perhaps I can help. I have something to show Amethyst and Dafydd in the Weapons Hall. Amethyst, perhaps you could bring your axe?"

I was already strapping Bane to my waist as I walked.

"Well, if you're sure, I have got some ideas for the kitchen…" Mum trailed off as she led Quartz into the kitchen area.

Ironfist gave us a wink and then led the way back past the central park area. The ferns looked eerily calm considering what had happened in the nearby chamber. At the enormous iron door to the Weapons Hall, Ironfist paused and raised his hand.

Chapter 22

The doors opened smoothly onto a large chamber. Axes and swords of all shapes and sizes lined the walls, stretching up into the ceiling. Each had a small plaque underneath It recording the name of the dwarf who had made it and the date. A ladder on wheels stood to one side; it was steam powered and allowed any dwarf to reach the highest weapons with the push of a button.

"These are the examples of work that every mastercraftsdwarf must submit before the Council agrees they can use the term 'dwarf-made' to describe their work. I believe yours is here Dafydd…" Ironfist looked around.

Dad walked over to a sword mounted on the wall near the door. He reached out a hand and caressed the blade. "I spent days working this piece, see the blue steel blade? And that pommel, that knot design took me almost as long as the blade," his eyes misted over as he remembered. Ironfist took the sword down and passed it around. I tested it. Perfectly balanced. Of course. Lorandir held it out at arm's length and agreed.

"This is an exquisite blade, Master Haernson, I can see where your daughter inherited her skills."

Dad smiled roundly at the compliment and puffed out his chest before taking the sword back and remounting it on the wall.

Ironfist continued through to a smaller chamber, "And here are our most famous blades. Weapons of note, stored here for posterity."

Dad looked around with a craftdwarf's interest at the blades. They ranged from simple single headed axes to more ornate blades. His eyes gleamed with pride at his own race's skill. The power of the ancient enchantments filled the air around us. I looked up in awe.

"I thought it was custom to pass weapons down through the generations?" Of course, Aloora knew about dwarven customs.

"In most cases, yes, but these weapons belong to families where the direct line has died out, or where a suitable heir could not be found. You see, these blades were forged far back with techniques lost to us today and some are, shall we say…temperamental about who wields them. They can be extremely dangerous in the wrong hands."

"Are any dragon blades?"

"Yes, there are some forged with dragon magic, when the magnificent creatures were not to be feared but lived alongside us. See over there, that is the blade commonly known as Dragonfire," Ironfist gestured to a sword mounted behind glass. Even through the protective case, I could feel the sense of danger and battle hunger coming from the long sword.

Aloora pressed her palm to the case eagerly. I knew she longed to feel the dragon magic imbued in the weapon first hand.

"But it is this I wanted to show you," Ironfist turned and moved to stand in front of another case. This one held a large double-headed axe. Runes were etched onto its blade and leather covered its haft. "According to the description, this is Bloodbane. Wielded by Lieffson, slayer of Meltar the furious, scourge of dwarfkind."

I looked at the axe with reverence. Every dwarf child knew the story of how Lieffson had killed the fire-breathing dragon millennia ago. With a single swing, he had cleaved the dragon's head from its body, or so the legend went. I had now seen several dragons and knew that either Lieffson had been incredibly strong, or the storytellers had embellished. A lot.

"You're related to Lieffson, aren't you?" Ironfist asked Dad with mild interest.

I didn't think Dad's chest could swell any further, but it did, "Indeed we are. I am proud to be able to count the glorious hero among my family's ancestors."

Ironfist nodded and unrolled a yellowed scroll on a small table to one side of the cave. We bent over the parchment. It was written in Dwarfish runes but the lines running down the scroll clearly showed a family tree. First, Ironfist showed us Dad's name at the very bottom of the scroll. Then he unrolled more and more of the ancient parchment.

I could see the joins where new pieces of vellum had been sewn together when the previous section ran out. He kept going until there was Lieffson's name next to a small but elaborate illustration of him decapitating a dragon.

"Huh, I always thought that was made up. All dwarves claim they're descended from some hero or another."

We looked up from the runes and turned back to the axe. My eyes sparkled. It was one thing having your Dad tell you bedtime stories about being related to famous heroes and another to know that it was real and there was the actual axe used in those stories.

"It looks like your axe," Lorandir turned to take in the double-headed axe hanging from my waist.

"Don't be ridiculous!" I gestured to the mounted weapon, "This is a great weapon imbued with ancient magic and wielded by a hero. Bane has been passed down in my family, but it's an ordinary enchanted axe."

"Is it now?" Ironfist's voice was quiet. We all turned to face him. He unlocked the cabinet holding Bloodbane and took out the blade. "What can you tell me about this?"

Dad took the weapon from the small dwarf and studied it carefully, lifting it this way and that in the light. After a minute, he whispered, "It can't be!"

"What?" Instead of answering, Dad passed the axe to me. I held it reverently. It was nicely balanced, but I couldn't sense any magic emanating from it. I traced the runes with my fingers. They had been etched in but not enchanted. "What the dzrak?"

"It appears that this is not Bloodbane," Ironfist paused for dramatic effect and raised his forefinger to emphasise his next words, "It's a fake!"

"Then where's the real Bloodbane? We need to tell someone about this! One of our most famous weapons has been stolen!"

Aloora put her small hand on my shoulder and met my gaze. It took me another few seconds for me to realise what she was getting at. "Wait a minute…you think that Bane is Bloodbane?! As in *the* axe that Lieffson used to kill a dragon?!"

"Yes! And when it touched the Meltar's blood, it became dragon forged! Imbued with strength beyond mere metal. Have you not noticed anything strange about the axe? Does it not respond to your will and lend you strength and power? Is it not imbued with more magic than you would expect from a pure dwarf-forged weapon?" Ironfist's voice was quiet but insistent.

I opened my mouth and closed it again. Yes, Bane did seem to be hungry for a fight and it certainly gave me strength in the duel with Mordred. Holy schiztz! Maybe it was Bloodbane. Ironfist nodded as if I'd spoken the revelation out loud before he continued, "But there is more. It is not widely known, but before Lieffson killed the dragon, he rode it. They had a bond until Meltar went mad and began killing indiscriminately," Ironfist shook his head sadly. "When the blade was dragon forged with Meltar's blood, it gained properties to enhance and amplify other magics. I don't know if you have felt that?"

I shook my head; it was a lot to take in. Ironfist didn't push it and carried on, "It seems that one of your ancestors decided to claim Bloodbane for their own rather than submitting it to the Council's care."

"How could they do that?" Dad asked with a frown.

"My guess, and it is only a guess, mind you, is that someone slipped in one day and swapped it out. Your relations have been on the Council several times over the past few hundred years…and there's so much magic in this room that no one has noticed that this is a copy."

Dad gave an impressed nod. But I could see where this was going. I put my hand protectively on my axe. I wasn't giving Bane up.

"Mr Haernson is a direct descendent of Lieffson, so technically he and his family line can wield the blade," Aloora sensed my concern, stepped forward and confronted the small Councilmember. I was glad someone knew dwarf lore, although I hadn't expected it to be the gnome. He held up his hands in a placating gesture.

"You misunderstand me. I am not going to tell anyone that this is not the real Bloodbane," he took the fake axe from my hand and replaced it in the cabinet. "The axe is clearly happy in the hands of the Haernson family and who am I to place a heroic weapon in a box when it so obviously wants to be used? I believe it is fated to be yours, Amethyst. Use it well and wisely. May your strikes be true and your enemies smoten."

I breathed a sigh of relief. Aloora stepped back beside me, still alert but not on the offensive. Her eyes drifted to the axe at my side. Now she knew it was dragon forged, I'd never hear the end of it. Ironfist nodded kindly and gestured for us to leave the armoury before he sealed the doors behind us.

"And there is one more thing…"

Chapter 23

Ironfist led the way along more tunnels to another, more secluded garden. The rain had stopped and weak autumn sunshine flooded the plants, reflecting off the droplets on their leaves as if they were jewels. Dotted among the leafy ferns and mossy boulders were rose quartz crystals. As we approached, they glowed a gentle pink. Ironfist smiled.

"They light up when those who are in love are near."

I blushed, gave Lorandir a secret look and held out my hand. He smiled down at me and took my palm. Bowing low, he pressed a kiss to my hand. It was still the most romantic gesture I'd ever experienced, and my stomach did a little flip at the warmth of his lips on my skin. Aloora rolled her eyes at his gallantry. Dad and Ironfist tactfully moved ahead. Ironfist touched the wall and suddenly the whole cave was filled with soft rosy light. I spun around, trying to take it all in. The dwarves had lined every wall with small rose quartz crystals. It was beautiful.

"Wow…" I had no words.

Ironfist nodded, "I am glad you like it. This is a garden of blessings and love. It has long been used to host weddings for loving dwarves." My eyes met the Councilmember's and I blinked stupidly. He carried on with the smoothness of a born diplomat, "Of course, we do not expect a decision right away, but I offer it to you with the blessing of the Council."

"What? But I'm not a dwarf!"

"Not in body perhaps, but in spirit…Amethyst you do not understand. You have built bridges with the elves, fought to save Avalon from destruction and despair and even today you slew a goliath. A thing nobody expected to see in this city! Dwarves are glad to count you among them."

"That's ridiculous, you saw them when I was receiving the medal. It was quiet."

"They were awed. No one knows what to expect! You are free from the constraints that we place upon ourselves. You choose to live with gnomes, humans, and elves where we isolate ourselves in our underground city. But times are changing. Oh, I know, the older dwarves may not like it, but you are showing the younger generation a different way of living. We would be honoured for our decorated hero and her elf prince to be wed here."

I took a step back, overcome by his speech, "Well, we, er, haven't had a lot of time to plan the wedding so we'll think about it."

Ironfist placed his right hand over his heart and bowed, "It is all I ask. Now, come, it is time to feast."

I hung back with Lorandir as the dwarf led Dad and Aloora out of the rose quartz chamber, explaining the significance of the crystals to the petite gnome as he went.

"It's really beautiful," I sighed.

"The second most beautiful thing here," he pushed back a lock of my hair that had twisted free from my plait. I gave him a playful swat on the arm. "If this is where you want us to be wed, we can tell Ironfist that we accept his offer."

"I want more time to think about it," I said truthfully. We had been engaged for such a short time and I wasn't sure what I wanted for our wedding. Apart from cake. There definitely had to be cake. I sighed, "Come on, let's go find the feast."

We didn't bother to go back to our quarters to get changed. My expensive dress was ruined, and I wanted to be comfortable if I had to endure more dark looks from elderly dwarves.

We found the feasting cave by following the stream of dwarves heading in the same direction. It looked like the entire city had been invited. Lorandir drew more attention than me thanks to his height and I heard some sniggers as he had to crouch yet again to navigate a tunnel that connected the city's main thoroughfare with the hall.

After Ironfist's speech, some of them sounded like good-natured laughs. Maybe the Councilmember was right. Maybe not everyone here hated us.

Once inside, I stopped, trying to take in the cacophony of sound and light. Huge tables were laid out like it was some sort of wizarding school. Chandeliers lit the room, carved from purple streaked lapis lazuli. The arches of the chandeliers ended with star shaped drops that provided the light for the cave.

I wracked my brains for the properties of the stone. It promoted harmony and bonds of friendship, as well as decreasing stress. I nodded appreciatively. It was a good choice for the feasting chamber. On the table were sweeping candelabras worked in glittering diamonds in geometric shapes. Smokeless candles sat snugly in the transparent candle holders and provided a cheery light over the long tables.

The tables themselves were already laden with hearty dwarven fare. Most of them ran lengthways in the rectangular cut cavern but one top table ran across the hall. The dwarves found themselves spots on cast iron chairs and settled down. Hundreds of chair legs scraped across the stone floor as they got comfortable. I searched for my family and Aloora from the spot where Lorandir and I stayed planted by the entrance. I caught Uncle Owain's gaze and he gave me a wave and pointed to the top table.

"There," Lorandir pointed to where Mum was standing and waving at the top table. Mortifying. I kept my eyes down and led the way to her side. Halfway along one of the enormous tables, an ancient dwarf waylaid us. Weighted down by formal armour and intricate charms, she appeared smaller than she actually was. She looked the elf up and down but didn't say anything.

I broke the silence and spoke in Dwarfish, "Hi Gran. How's the mine?"

"Hail well, old woman." I winced at Lorandir's attempt at Dwarfish. It wasn't awful but he was used to the flowing speech of elves. Dwarfish normally required the speakers to sound like they were arguing, preferably while swilling rocks around their mouths.

"So this is the elf? What do you see in him?" Gran ignored my fiancé. Elven glamour didn't work on her.

"Well…I love him."

"Psff. Love. In my day, you married for the size of the mine and hoped you'd rub along well enough."

"We really should be going…" I tried to sidestep the old dwarf, but she cut me off with a well-placed mining tool to my ribs. One of my cousins tried to help by grabbing her arm. He got an elbow in the stomach for his trouble.

"He treats you well?"

"He does. Honestly, it's good. Don't even worry about it."

"Hmmf," she switched to English so he could understand, "I don't understand your choice, but I won't oppose it. Times are changing and even us dwarves must move with them I suppose." My mouth dropped open in disbelief at Gran's unexpected blessing. "But, if he ever hurts you, I will personally skewer his brozzards from his body and barbeque them."

"OK, thanks Gran." This time I managed to extricate us from the conversation, and we hurried to the top table.

Chapter 24

We sat down and I grabbed for a large pewter jug. I poured it into a silver goblet, hoping it was alcohol. The dwarven gods were with me. I sloshed the rich, red wine into my goblet and then offered it to my fiancé. After a fortifying sip, I looked at the table more closely.

Huge legs of honey-glazed ham and mouth-watering pink beef sat on silver platters. I recognised traditional dwarven stews topped with meatballs and a green vegetable dish I could never remember the name of. There were massive pies with thick golden pastry concealing rich fillings. My stomach rumbled in appreciation. I took another swig of my drink to quiet it and surreptitiously reached for the crusty bread roll that someone had thoughtfully placed on the small, polished silver plates to the left of each place setting.

I was halfway through the bread when a Councilmember towards the middle of the top table stood and asked for quiet. Instead of tapping a fork to a glass, she banged her axe on the table until everyone was looking in her direction.

"Friends! We are here today to celebrate those who have shown their bravery twice over. Not only are they heroes of the Battle of Avalon, but today they defeated the goliath that breached our city!"

A cheer went up around the hall, accompanied by the sound of thousands of dwarves banging their weapons on their own tables. Euan stood and gave a bow with a flourish. Dirtbiter's scowl looked almost like a smile.

"Today's victory did not come without cost, so let us raise a glass to our brethren who died a noble death and are surely dining in the halls of our ancestors tonight!"

Respectful cheers accompanied by sobs sounded as the dwarves raised their drinking horns and goblets to the fallen. The dwarf motioned for quiet again.

"Out of all our heroes, I want to give special thanks to the one who killed the beast; Amethyst Haernson!"

Another cry went up. I felt my cheeks burn at the attention and waved shyly as I swallowed a piece of bread. Please don't let me have to give a speech. I waved nervously. Fortunately, the Councilmember just smiled politely and continued.

"Thanks to her efforts and her expertise in metalwork, being the first dwarf in living memory to create a draconic piece of jewellery, the Council has decided to grant her the distinction of the hallmark of 'dwarf-made'." There was a collective intake of breath from the room. With a slight bow to me, the Councilmember gestured to a dwarf who had been waiting behind the table. He walked over and presented me with a small leather bag. I looked around. There was an air of expectation. I was clearly supposed to open it.

I loosened the thin leather thong holding it shut and reached inside. My hand closed on a thin piece of metal about three inches long. I retrieved it and held it up. It was a small rectangular pressart or stamp. On the base of the round rod was the crest of the Dwarven Arms Council. The hallmark that would show everyone that my jewellery was considered high enough quality to be known as dwarf-made. The hallmark that would add at least twenty per cent to my prices. Tears filled my eyes.

Then I felt the anger rising. It didn't seem fair. What about other half-dwarves? I opened my mouth to protest, not sure what I was going to say. Mum elbowed me in the ribs and the Councilmember kept going.

"In making this decision, the Council was advised of how passionately Ms Haernson asked for this honour to be considered for all dwarf descendants," she paused and nodded to Ironfist, who smiled enigmatically. "And so, *we*," she emphasised that and looked meaningfully at the eldest members of the Council who met her gaze then looked away, "have made the decision that any descendant up to a quarter-dwarf may be considered for this hallmark and judged on the quality of their work rather than the purity of their blood."

Half of the hall burst into raucous applause at this. The other half sat stunned for a second before joining in more slowly. My Gran was in the second half of the room.

"And now…we feast!" The Councilmember lifted her huge golden goblet and took a deep drink. She wiped the froth of the beer from her top lip and sat down to the loudest applause yet at the mention of food.

I'd been to a few dwarf feasts in my time and this one was just like the ones I remembered from my childhood, only on a much larger scale. Everyone reached for the heaped central dishes at the same time before laughing and stepping back. Someone would become the de facto carver of the meats and pies and cut them into thick slices with sharp carving knives before passing them out onto upheld plates.

Lorandir sat back politely, waiting to be offered something. I picked up his plate as well as my own and held them out towards the tempting dishes, knowing that if I didn't, neither of us would get any food. When they were both laden to the point where anything added to the plate would have fallen off, I placed the metal plates back in front of us. Lorandir studied the cutlery appreciatively.

"These are really well made."

"Of course they are! It's part of the training of any forge master to make exquisite cutlery. Now I daresay these will be a special ceremonial set for the occasion, but any metal-working dwarf will make excellent cutlery," Dad was in his element here. He held a fork up to the light and studied the markings as best as he could without his jeweller's loupe. "If I'm not mistaken, these are pure silver and five hundred years old. And see this marking here? That's the Medal of Honour. This will be the flatware brought out at every ceremony. Not the original cutlery used at the first ceremony, of course, but a worthy replica."

"Dad! Let Lorandir eat!" I could sense he was about to start a lecture on the finer points of metal working and our food would get cold.

Dad nodded and turned back to his own plate, piled high with meats and slices of pie. He ate with relish as whenever

Mum tried traditional dwarven recipes at home, they invariably went wrong. He constantly told her to stick to human food, which he enjoyed as well, but she kept trying.

I had just put a hefty chunk of chewy beef into my mouth when a cough behind me told me someone was there. I turned and took in the smiling face of the Councilmember who had given the speech. Ironfist stood next to her, smiling politely. I chewed furiously, trying to empty my mouth before I spoke.

"Congratulations Ms Haernson, Master Ironfist was vociferous about your abilities and your sense of justice. We owe you a great debt."

I finally swallowed the piece of beef. I opened my mouth and coughed. I'd misjudged the size of the morsel and it had got lodged in my throat. I turned back for my wine to help wash it down and spilled the cup over the table. Lorandir patted me forcefully on the back. I coughed up the gobbet of meat onto the floor by the Councilmember's feet. Mum found a linen serviette and dabbed at the spilled wine. Without missing a beat, Ironfist picked my goblet up from the floor and refilled it.

"Don't even worry about it," my voice was hoarse, and I took a long drink of the rich wine.

"Indeed," the Councilmember arched a bushy eyebrow, "I am Master Helgdotjr. I would be honoured to commission a piece from you. I have been seeking a new cuff for a while and nothing has seemed right. Perhaps I could ask you to send me through some sketches?"

I swallowed hard. This was a big deal. "Of course, I'll get something over to you er...do you have an e-mail?"

Helgdotjr smiled and handed me a business card, "Naturally. And I hear congratulations are in order," she looked from me to Lorandir. "You are a most unusual dwarf, Amethyst Haernson. I look forward to seeing what you come up with." The Councilmember glided off to talk to another medal recipient. I watched her leather skirt sway as she walked away.

"Wow!"

"Well done, Amethyst! Freya's approval does not come lightly," Ironfist clapped me on the shoulder and then followed his fellow Councilmember.

I could feel the grin stuck on my face. Dad smiled back at me and Lorandir whispered, "Well done!" in my ear. This had to be one of the best days of my life. Servers came in to whisk away plates and replace the central dishes with vast mountains of dessert. I caught sight of a gooey chocolate cake covered with dark chocolate sauce between a pile of stuffed pastries and a mess of fruit and cream. It could possibly be *the* best day of my life…so far.

Chapter 25

Morning came and I could hear Dad clattering about in the kitchen. I groaned. I'd had too much wine last night. And the mead afterwards had been a bad idea. I pulled the covers over my head and tried to go back to sleep, but it was no good. With another groan, I got up. Lorandir came into the room from the kitchen. He was already washed and dressed, having stopped drinking after his second glass of wine. Bloody sensible elf. He produced a plate of sausages with hash browns and my grumpiness eased slightly. I used my fingers to grab a sausage and then dropped it. I sucked my index finger.

"Careful, they're hot."

"Thanks for the warning!" I pulled myself out of bed and headed to the bathroom. When I got back, Lorandir had gone, but he'd left the food on the bedside table. I ate with the fluffy towel wrapped around me. The greasy food helped to settle my churning stomach and I got dressed quickly before heading in search of caffeine.

Dad had tinkered with the coffee machine, so it now whirred and sputtered ominously in the kitchen. He couldn't help himself. I tentatively pushed a button and stepped back as steam rose out from a newly installed vent system. The machine let out a harsh sucking sound before glugging out a cappuccino. The milky foam on top oozed over the sides of the mug slightly. I took a sip and nodded to myself. It was a decent cup of coffee.

"Not bad for your old man, hey?"

"Good work Dad."

He stroked his beard, satisfied with his work. Sometimes I forgot how good dwarves were at quaffing alcohol. He was barely affected. There was a loud knock on the door before it banged open and my Uncles entered cheerfully. They were equally unaffected by the copious amounts of booze imbibed last night. Uncle Owain was holding a small green wyrm, who instantly jumped out of his hands and ran towards Errol. My dragon-like pet opened his sleepy eyes and looked at the newcomer warily. A small growl escaped from his throat.

"Ah, it's nice to see them getting along." The young wyrm started pouncing on the older creature. Errol opened his mouth and breathed out a spurt of fire. It seemed to egg the smaller wyrm on. Errol grunted irritably and turned his back. "Young Sharptooth here needs socialising, and I couldn't leave him at the farm for a whole night on his own." Behind Owain's back, Dylan rolled his eyes.

"Congratulations, Amethyst," Dylan stepped forward and enveloped me in a huge bear hug. "Here, I brought you some of my famous cake for the journey home. It's a shame we can't all stay longer, but we have to be getting back - the wyrms need their care."

I took the proffered tin of cake and opened it. The haze of brandy fumes made me blink and cough. I closed it again quickly as my head started to reel anew. "Thanks."

Uncle Owain gave me another bear hug, "I'm glad we got to see you properly before we went. I suppose the next time we're all together will be at your wedding! Any ideas when you're having it?"

"Er…" No. I had no idea.

"Well, let us know as soon as you can in case we have to make wyrm sitter arrangements. Sharptooth! Come!"

The young wyrm jumped over Errol happily while my lazy pet blew smoke rings for him to catch. My Uncle tried to get the green wyrm to pay attention to him by calling again. When that didn't work, he strode over and grabbed him mid-leap. The wyrm showed its annoyance by biting Owain's hand.

"Ouch! You little rascal. Well, we'd better be off. See you soon."

Dylan shook his head at his partner's tolerance for wyrms and followed behind. I handed the cake tin to Mum as she bustled out of her room towing her large suitcase behind her.

"Really Dafydd! I don't know why we have to set off so early!"

"I want to beat the traffic and the sun's already up."

Mum sighed and made herself a green tea rather than face the noisy coffee machine, "So is everyone else ready?"

I nodded. It wouldn't take long to shove my things into my suitcase, especially since I didn't have to worry about spoiling my fancy dress and Lorandir was already packed. "Schiztz. Aloora."

"Get her up then!" Dad was already fussing around the suitcases stacked by the door.

I walked down the corridor and knocked on my friend's door. No response. I pushed it open, "Aloora, time to get up."

She groaned and rolled over under the thick covers. I tried again. I was rewarded with another groan and this time some words accompanied it, "Go away!"

"It's time to get up if you want any breakfast."

"Don't talk to me about food!"

"Dad's going to leave you here if you don't get ready."

"Good, now go away."

"I'll put the lights on."

"You're a monster!"

I turned on the crystal lights at their dimmest setting, revealing a trail of clothes strewn over the floor. Aloora pulled the covers over her head. I marched over to her bed and yanked them off. She screwed her face up at me, "Alright, alright, I'm getting up."

"I'm coming back in ten minutes so don't go back to sleep."

Aloora waved me away. I crossed over to my room and threw my things into my suitcase. I debated trying to fit in one of the beautiful glowing lamps, but decided against it. They'd definitely notice if one of the matching sets of bedside lights was missing. Instead, I zipped up my case and dragged it out to the front door before going back to check on my friend.

She had got dressed and was tugging a comb through her short hair in front of the polished onyx mirror. Her features looked even more delicate reflected in the flattering sheet of rock and I could hardly see the dark smudges under her eyes.

I opened my mouth to speak. She held out her hand to stop me and shook her head. "Not until I've had my coffee."

"As you wish," I gave a mock bow and went to make her a cup.

When I got back to her room, the sea of clothes was gone, and she was sitting on her suitcase trying to get it to close enough so she could zip it up. I handed her the coffee, "Here, let me."

We exchanged places and my weight forced the sides of the case together so we could get it done up. She grabbed the case and pulled it along to the lounge area like it had personally affronted her while she sipped the bitter-smelling coffee.

"Nice of you to join us," Dad joked.

Aloora gave him a look but mercifully kept quiet. I didn't want an entire day stuck in the car with an argument going on. Ironfist's guards were on hand to escort us out. Today they were wearing suits rather than kilts, but their axes were still on display at their hips. The lead guard nodded and hefted our bags into a waiting carriage.

We retraced our journey from when we'd first entered, around the park and to the gigantic doors. There weren't many people about just after sunrise the night after a big feast, but the dwarves that were around stood respectfully to the side of the roadways as we passed. Then they started cheering and clapping. Lorandir waved with the practised elegance of a born prince. Errol curled around his shoulders added to the effect of an ethereal elf.

"Wave," he urged me out of the side of his mouth, never losing his serene smile, "They're cheering for you."

I frowned in disbelief but waved my hand in what I imagined was an imitation of the Queen. The crowd went wild. I grinned at them. They really were cheering me…well us. The euphoria of acceptance went to my head, and I stood in the cart, waving manically. The dwarves cheered even louder at my appreciation.

Then the cart hit a bump on the cave floor, and I fell onto my arse in the footwell. I glared at the driver, but he stared straight ahead. Titters of laughter mixed with the cheering. Lorandir offered me his hand. His face showed concern, but I caught the twinkle of amusement in his eyes. I pulled myself up, my cheeks red with embarrassment. When the dwarves saw me again, they cheered. This time, I stayed seated while I waved.

At the huge metal doors, Ironfist and Helgdotjr were waiting for us in leather vests, which were less decorated than what they'd worn for the Council ceremony. Ironfist beckoned to Aloora, and she climbed down from the carriage, stifling a yawn with her hand.

As he whispered in her ear, Helgdotjr gave the rest of us a formal Council goodbye, which was wordy and polite. After she finished, she clasped each of us by the forearm and wished us safe travels. Aloora unloaded her suitcase from the cart and then gave us each a hug.

"Sorry I can't drive you back Dafydd, the Magical Liaison Office has asked me to stay on. They're sending a couple of people to look into the goliath attack."

Dad stroked his beard and tried to keep the relieved smile off of his face. Aloora stepped back and stood next to the two dwarves. She looked a little out of place, dressed in a jersey dragon print dress and standing a couple of inches taller than our hosts. Ironfist gave us each a traditional goodbye. As he leaned forward and clasped my forearm, he whispered, "Don't forget to think about our offer of a wedding venue."

Chapter 26

The car journey was just as long going back. I dozed in the back seat alongside Errol until we stopped for lunch at a proper pub. I had been looking forward to some decent food, but my mood quickly soured after I found a discarded tabloid paper with the headline; *Is Amethyst pregnant?*

I scanned the article, which was full of conjecture and speculation about my slightly rounded tummy. It was accompanied by a photo of me walking down one of Cardiff's shopping streets with Mum, while I stuffed a cake into my mouth. We both had shopping bags slung over our arms and the caption underneath the picture wondered if we had bought baby clothes.

There was a close up of my stomach with an arrow and the words '*boy or girl?*' printed next to it. The article ended by saying that '*Amethyst declined to comment on whether or not she was having a baby*'. Of course I hadn't commented! No one had bloody called me! There were then some quotes from people who had allegedly met me. I scowled as I saw a smiling photo of the greasy-haired teenager who had asked me if I was pregnant. So that was where this had started.

Was this going to be my life now? Forever in gossip papers for the slightest comment that a stranger made. It wasn't what I'd expected my life to be or even what I wanted. Lorandir read the article over my shoulder and gave me a hug.

"Don't worry, I'll get some of Morty's people on it, they handle press all the time."

I hugged him back. At least there was one thing I was sure of; I wanted to choose to spend my life with him.

"Ame, is it true?"

I turned to see Mum's eyes pooling with tears. Dad spat out his mouthful of warm beer. I was sure it was intentional that he sprayed Lorandir before he blustered his congratulations.

Back in the car after assuring Mum that I was not actually pregnant, I wanted a distraction from the disturbing headlines. We played I-spy for a bit until Mum chose "Horizon" as a word. An hour spent trying to guess things that begin with an aitch soured the game a lot. In the end, we were quiet, watching the scenery while seventies rock played through the main car speakers.

Mum and Dad dropped me and Lorandir off in the carpark of our apartment building and drove off to spend another night at Lorandir's place. Mum had mentioned wedding dress shopping in the morning and then had got overexcited when I mentioned that Madam Tinselle had offered to design me a custom dress. Hopefully that would keep her occupied.

Lorandir and I crammed into the small lift with our suitcases in tow and travelled to our floor in silence. I unlocked our front door and gave it a shove. Being a fire door, it was heavy. Being cut a couple of millimetres too large for the doorframe, it stuck. A bang sounded close to my ears and reams of paper string flew at my face. Errol let out a bolt of flame in shock. Marco jumped to one side to avoid the flames and the fire alarm started beeping. Marco grabbed a white tea towel and waved it half-heartedly at the small plastic container that chirruped loudly. A rhythmic banging from upstairs told us that someone else had heard the fire alarm and wanted us to keep it down. Eventually, the alarm dulled to an intermittent beep. Marco let off another party popper.

"Welcome back! You are 'ere at last!"

"Good to see you too Marco," I followed him into our living space and stopped.

The entire room seemed to have become the sort of thing you see on TV detective stories where they have a cork board crime wall mapping out a murder. Except here, every available space in our lounge had been taken up with wedding pictures.

"Do you like it?"

"What is it?"

"It's a mood board for your wedding! It's good, no?"

"Er…"

"See, here I 'ave made a start but, there is space for you to add pictures that you like. You can cut them from wedding magazines."

Marco fiddled with a board and I realised that the white tea towel was, in fact, a fabric swatch of some type of lace. I stared.

"Er…I haven't even looked at any magazines."

"I 'ave bought some for you," he thrust a stack of hefty magazines covered with bridal beauty and ornate flowers at me. With horror, I noticed that one of them was for pregnant brides. I stepped forward and sank onto our sofa.

"It's lovely Marco, thank you," Lorandir gave him a genuine smile before pulling him into a hug. Marco beamed at the compliment and sat down next to me, careful not to wrinkle his perfectly creased linen trousers.

"This is a lot of information."

Marco nodded, "Yes, that is why it is good to start early. Now what theme did you 'ave in mind?"

"Er…"

His face fell a little, "OK, 'ow about a budget, 'ow much do you 'ave to spend?"

"Er…" I thought about my savings account, somewhat depleted after my shop had been burned down and I hadn't relaunched my collection yet. I'd made a few sales off the online shop that Aloora had set up for me, but I really needed to keep what was in my account to make sure I could pay my share of our rent. It was less than you'd expect to pay for a flat in the popular Cardiff Bay thanks to dragons colonising the city last year and driving the rent prices down, but it was still a fair chunk of money each month.

"What's the normal budget?" Lorandir asked.

"Well, according to the magazines, twenty thousand is a good amount, but I don't know if that will get you the wedding of your dreams."

My mouth dropped open at the eye watering sum of twenty thousand pounds. Right now, my dreams consisted of not spending that amount of money. "We could put down a deposit on a house for that much!"

Marco raised an eyebrow at me, "Where is the romance in an 'ouse? Now look at this, see 'ow the lace shimmers over the satin…" His eyes misted over as he ran a manicured hand along the glossy page he was showing me. "What did you think for a dress? I can see you in this one…"

I stared at the poufy meringue-like dress he was pointing at. If I wore that, I would look like something that should be in a cake shop.

"Er, Madam Tinselle is making my dress, so we don't need to worry about that."

If I'd thought that the name of the fashion designer would help, I was wrong. Marco let out a theatrical gasp and clutched his hands to his chest. I swear he almost did a genuflection at her name.

"Then your wedding must be more perfect if it is to host a Tinselle creation! What do you think of these napkins?"

Marco held up two identical white napkins in front of my face. I blinked at them. "Er, I like that one?"

He rewarded me with a beaming smile, "I knew it! Of course you would want the fresh snow colour. I don't know why I even thought of the apple blossom."

I squinted at the two napkins. Nope. They were exactly the same colour. An idea popped into my head. "Er, Marco, you're so much better at all this wedding stuff than me. Would you like to be my wedding planner?"

"Santa Maria! Of course I will! It will be perfecto!" He swept me into a large hug and then did the same to my fiancé.

"Now, we 'ave to decide on a theme…and a date…and the invitations…"

"How about you come up with some options for us to look at?"

"But of course!" He started grabbing magazines and flicking through them at top speed.

"I'm just going to…" I backed away to my bedroom. Marco didn't notice me leaving the lounge. I dumped my suitcase in a corner of my room and fell backwards onto the bed. Lorandir joined me.

"You've made him very happy."

I smiled, "I know."

"You do realise what you're letting yourself in for though?"

My smile faded. Schiztz. Marco was going to be high maintenance.

Chapter 27

I wasn't wrong. The next day, Marco presented me with a list of potential venues, caterers, and florists that he wanted us to visit. He had the next months all planned out. He had also created a scrapbook full of theme ideas. It was covered with lace and had Amethyst and Lorandir written on it in flowing calligraphy underneath pictures of us that he'd cut out from newspapers.

There was a huge heart surrounding us made out of what looked like bark. I had no idea how he had found the time to make the scrapbook and still get enough rest to look like something out of a fashion magazine. The second we had emerged from my room, he had thrust the book at me along with a cup of thick espresso coffee and a plate of homemade cannoli.

Now he stared at me expectantly from the bean bag chair. Somehow, he still managed to look elegant while lying almost horizontally and sipping his own tiny mug of black espresso.

I flicked through the book. There was a diary marked out in neat rows at the back.

"But there are no free weekends at all!"

"You can 'ave free time when you're married!" Marco gave Lorandir a look that said he felt sorry that the elf was marrying someone so oblivious to the nuances of wedding planning.

The doorbell rang. Marco extracted himself from the beanbag with graceful speed and headed for the door. I eyed him suspiciously. My fears were realised as I heard Mum's voice in the hall. I closed my eyes and took a breath.

"Darling! Marco's told me all about his ideas for your big day! It sounds wonderful."

"Ye-es."

"Well, what's this I hear about you not wanting to look at venues?"

I'd lost, but there was such a thing as going down fighting, "It's not that I don't want to…"

"Excellent," Mum cut me off before I could finish. She rubbed her hands together in satisfaction before accepting Marco's offer of a coffee. "We've got to get started! He's managed to get an appointment at the most exclusive hotel in the city. Really Marco, I don't know how you did it."

I looked to Dad for help. He studiously avoided my gaze and took a sip of his own Italian blend. Traitor.

"Well, I'd better be off then. I said I'd meet Gunther for a pint…" Dad trailed off at the look of disapproval on Mum's face, "I'll just get in the car."

"Oh no you don't, Dafydd! Really, it's bad enough that you don't want to help your only daughter look at wedding venues, you're going to leave us stranded! No. I will drive. You can make your own way to meet Gunther."

"I can't believe you're not coming with us Dad! I am your only daughter!" I tried to keep the smile from my face as I rubbed it in. It was petty, I know, but I didn't see why he could get out of it and I couldn't. Dad's face flushed bright red, and he turned for the door. I didn't quite catch the Dwarfish swear word he used, but its meaning was clear.

I chuckled to myself as I strapped on Bane, I mean Bloodbane, and pushed my enchanting goggles into my bushy hair. They completed my steampunk style look well and the brown lenses set off the bronze studs in my corset top. Mum sucked her lips in at my choice and protested at my taking a weapon with me, but I told her, "No weapon, no wedding planning," and she contented herself with a disapproving look.

Lorandir was more circumspect and left his own sword safe in my room, but then he had magic.

Mum downed her coffee, grabbed her handbag like it was a shield between her and my fashion choices and stood up briskly, "Let's get going!"

She opened the door and almost bumped into the tall figure of King Morthimas. The elf blinked and steadied Mum to stop her from falling as she executed an abrupt stop. She looked like she was about to faint with delight at the sight of the royal elf.

"Morty?" Lorandir's voice made it clear he was surprised to see his cousin. "What are you doing here?"

"Cousin! I'm so glad I found you! I wanted to talk to you about the wedding."

Mum's eyes immediately brightened, and she pulled the King inside our flat. "What a coincidence! We were about to go look at venues today, why don't you come in your majesty? Is that what I should call you?"

"Please, call me Morty," he replied suavely as he escorted her back into the living room. Two members of the Elven High Council entered behind him, keeping as far away from the walls as possible. They perched on the sofa stiffly and declined Marco's offer of coffee and pastries.

I moved a pile of lace and flowers on the shabby chic wooden table and leaned against it. Lorandir joined me, his arms folded as he tried to work out what his cousin was up to.

The King coughed and sipped his cappuccino delicately. His nose wrinkled at the bitter taste, but he smiled and thanked Marco before setting the plain white cup on an end table. "So, how is everyone?"

"Morty…" there was an edge to my fiancé's voice.

"Yes, yes, alright, I'll get straight to it. I've come to formally offer the Evergreen Palace for your wedding. Of course, I know it's a lot to think about but look," with a twist of his hands, a holographic model of Breconia, the elven city, appeared in front of him. It was like a 3D version of a map as he manipulated the image until the huge palace tree was the only part of the forest city visible. "As you can see, here is a perfect place for the ceremony…and it will be easier to control the press if you're in our lands…"

The magic vision zoomed in until it showed the large hall at the base of the tree. I saw Mum nodding along and leaning forward as the King continued the strange presentation.

I looked at Lorandir. He was frowning slightly as his cousin enthused about the spacious hall, the leafy forest and the elven catering options. I hadn't wanted to get married in the beautiful cavern of Jarnstradr, but had Lorandir always dreamed of a traditional elven wedding?

"It's…nice," I whispered. I thought of our time together at the Equinox Ball. The Evergreen Palace had been the place where we'd first got together, and it was beautiful…even if the forest contained dangerous beasts and the elves weren't exactly welcoming to outsiders. And there was always the risk of dragons gate-crashing the wedding. "If you want to, we can get married there."

Of course, the other elves could hear me, but the two Councilmembers stayed still, their faces displaying no emotion. The King tactfully ignored our conversation and focused on answering Mum's many questions about parking and accommodation.

"It's nice," Lorandir started. Morthimas gave up all pretence of not eavesdropping and beamed at his cousin. "It's nice but, I don't think it's really right for me and Amethyst."

I sighed and squeezed his hand.

"Alright then, in that case, perhaps we can join you today?" Morty clapped his hands together, not seeming the least disappointed that we hadn't chosen the palace. I narrowed my eyes at Morty's back as we left. He seemed suspiciously upbeat about us turning down the venue and coming with us today.

Chapter 28

My feet ached by the time we finally sat down in the Dragon's Head coffee shop at four p.m. I considered taking off my gothic style boots and rubbing my toes, but the sturdy laces were a pain to undo, and I couldn't remember if I'd picked matching socks. Instead, I contented myself with leaning back in the soft fabric chair and stretching my legs out. It had been a full day.

We had seen two hotels, a florist and a cake maker in less than six hours. Marco had a black fountain pen in his hand and was monopolising the rustic style table as he ticked boxes in his scrapbook and scrawled a line through something else on his list. Mum and Morthimas studied it over his shoulder, Mum pointed out something on the page. The two Councilmembers had their own table adjacent to ours. They sipped herbal tea and pointedly ignored the stares of the other customers who weren't immune to the elven glamour. I thanked Gunther silently for the anti-glamour charm he'd given me. The elves were still inhumanly attractive, but at least I wasn't falling over myself trying to buy them drinks.

Brinda, the owner of my favourite coffee shop, bustled up to the table with our second hot drink order and a plate piled high with her signature gooey chocolate brownies. Reluctantly, Marco packed the ornate scrapbook away into his leather man bag to make space for the drinks.

I took a sip, then heaped a forkful of the delicious brownie into my mouth. I almost sighed with pleasure, "These brownies are heaven. I must have tasted ten different cakes today and this is without a doubt the best thing I've tried. It's a shame we can't get Brinda to cater the wedding."

Mum and Marco looked at me with twin expressions of surprise on their faces.

"That's an excellent idea, Ame!"

"No need to sound so surprised," I grumbled. No one heard me; Mum was already calling Brinda back over. Even Lorandir sat forward. He had spent the day being patiently appreciative and subtly pulling Marco back from some of his more outlandish ideas, whereas Morthimas seemed determined to egg him on.

I repressed a shudder at the memory of the rainbow feather boas Marco had been contemplating for centrepieces. To be fair to him, the King had offered to take care of all flowers and decorations as a wedding gift to his cousin. Now I just had to hope that Marco didn't get too carried away with access to exotic elven blooms. Morthimas had already begun sketching out designs, one of which seemed to have an oversized venus fly trap looming out of it.

Mum explained to Brinda that we were getting married, and she wondered if the Dragon's Head did catering. She made it sound like her own wedding, so she had to go through the request a second time as Brinda tried to work out who was actually getting married out of the four of us. When she realised it was me and Lorandir, her face brightened.

"Of course, I can cater a wedding for my best customer! And I will get another signed photo for the wall, yes?" she indicated the picture Mum had sent her. It was the same dzraking photo everyone had of me and Lorandir after the dzraking dragon had destroyed the castle.

Mum agreed instantly and started talking about the menu. Brinda told a harassed looking young man to handle the end of day service while she discussed catering with Mum and Marco. The first time they looked to me for input, I decided to put my foot down, "The only thing I want at my wedding is some of your amazing sausage baps and piles of these brownies."

Marco rolled his eyes at me, and they carried on talking. Lorandir squeezed my hand comfortingly.

"Why don't we go for a walk while you finalise the details?" he suggested. I don't think I'd ever loved him more than the moment he got me out of wedding planning.

The King, Mum and Marco, all waved me away and bowed their head over the scrapbook, which had reappeared. I thought I heard the phrase "six tiers…" as we left the café. I shook my head.

Lorandir took my arm in his and we decided to meander over to Bute Park. The late September sun was hanging low in the sky, and it was a mild day with no breeze to bring a chill to the air.

We crossed the road and walked past Cardiff Castle, where a few visitors were lazily leaving and trying to decide between going home or sampling one of the city's restaurants. I side-stepped a member of a re-enactment group dragging three long spears behind him as he headed for home, still dressed up in medieval gear, complete with a chain mail shirt and shiny helmet.

"I wonder what it's like in there now?" I mused. The castle had undergone significant rebuilding after the red dragon had destroyed part of it.

"Shall we find out?" Lorandir steered us to the ticket office just inside the large gate. He took out his wallet, "Two please."

The elderly man in the ticket office looked at us and checked the time on his watch, "The castle's already closed for the day and we're closing the grounds in fifteen minutes…"

"Alright, how much for just the grounds?"

"Tell you what, you look like a nice couple…why don't you just go in today, my treat."

We thanked the man and he winked and motioned us into the castle grounds. Lorandir replaced my arm in the crook of his elbow, and we headed into the grounds. The ruined keep stared down at us from the top of its steep hill. To the left, the main castle looked like a cross between a vast manor house and a fairy-tale castle. The newly rebuilt brick shone a pinkish red against the muted, older building. We headed towards it, crossing the green grass slowly.

"Do you remember?" Lorandir whispered.

I swallowed and nodded. I remembered. I remembered a lot about the day that a dragon had awakened. The terror of being captured by a cult. The horror of seeing a huge reptile devour people in front of me. And…our first kiss. That was the memory I had most of our time here. I looked up at the tall elf. He was looking down at me with a sparkle in his eyes that made a wave of heat rush through me. I raised my face as he bent his head towards mine. As our lips met, it felt right.

"You know, I'd like wherever we get married to be somewhere meaningful to us, you and me, not our families or the dwarves or the elves. Something that's us," I tested the waters.

Lorandir looked at me. His green eyes seemed to read my mind. "Somewhere like where we had our first kiss."

I gave him a lopsided smile, and he returned it before bending to kiss me again. A cough interrupted us, and we broke apart.

"It's closing time, if you would…" a spotty teenager pointed to the gate before walking away to corral more visitors to the exit. On our way out past the gatehouse, I asked for their wedding brochure. The guard gave us another wink as he handed over a printed piece of cardboard.

I studied the glossy brochure as we continued our walk. We were almost past the carved animals that lined the stone wall between the castle and the park entrance when I got that same prickle between my shoulder blades I'd had before. I stopped and looked around. I couldn't see anything out of the ordinary. The pavement was clear of pedestrians now. We were alone in the shade cast by the trees and the back of the castle.

"What is it?" Lorandir asked, straining his superior senses to find what had unsettled me.

"Nothing, just a feeling…"

I forced myself to carry on walking. Then I heard the scrape of stone on stone.

Chapter 29

I swung round and my mouth dropped open. One of the carved animals pulled itself from the wall. Cement dust trickled down the stones as it pulled up one paw, then another. It studied each limb, twisting its head from side to side.

"Schiztz!"

Its head snapped round at the sound of my voice. It opened its mouth wide and bared its fangs at us. Double schiztz. I recognised the twisted face of the carved baboon. I had always thought that particular sculpture was especially creepy. Now it pulled itself from the wall. Its glass eyes glowed a dull red as they focused on us. Its tail whipped up behind it. Triple schiztz.

"Run!" Lorandir gathered magic to his hands and aimed a blast of power at the creature as he ran backwards with the sure-footedness of an elf. I risked a glance over my shoulder. With monkey-like agility, the stone baboon dodged the blow. It raced along the parapet of the wall with ease, snarling horribly. It bounded over the other, still static, carved creatures. The baboon was gaining on us.

We skidded through the wrought iron gates into Bute Park. Lorandir was ahead of me. I looked again. Nothing followed us through the gates. I felt a swirl of that same tainted magic I'd experienced before. I pulled my crafting goggles down over my eyes. A crunch made me look up. The baboon had scaled the wall that separated the castle grounds from the park.

Under my goggles, it glowed a painfully familiar rusty red colour. A thin strand of the magic headed away from the baboon and further into the park. Before I could follow the trail, the possessed monkey leapt down and headed straight for me. I unhooked Bloodbane from my belt and readied myself. I blocked its first jump with my axe.

It switched tactics and made a grab for my boot. I felt the amethyst round my neck heat up as it leant me protection against the evil magic. I willed the jewel's power to lend me strength as I lifted my other foot and stamped down hard on the thing's head. The impact with the stone creature made me grunt. I hoped I hadn't broken my metatarsal. It released my foot and leapt again.

A ball of magic hit it in the side. It staggered then turned. With a guttural shriek, it headed for Lorandir.

"No!" I sprinted to help the elf. The unnatural creature pounced and hit my fiancé square in the chest. Lorandir fell backwards, his arms up, trying to fend off the baboon's fangs as it mauled at its face. He hit the ground hard, unable to break his fall with an angry stone monster attacking him. I heard him gasp for breath.

I swung my axe hard, aiming for its neck. The baboon shuddered as the heavy blade connected. It gave a shriek and turned to me. I pulled my axe free and readied myself. It tensed and sprung upwards.

I used Bloodbane like a baseball bat and hit the creature square in its flank. The baboon made an angry noise as it went flying towards a tree. I stared after it. There was no way I should have been able to hit a piece of solid stone hard enough to launch it twenty feet across the park.

I gave a silent thank you to my trusty axe as I heard the satisfying thunk of the baboon colliding with a sturdy oak. Before it could recover, I muttered the Dwarfish word to activate Bloodbane's shield and bent down to Lorandir. Blood soaked his fitted t-shirt turning the soft mossy green a dark red. A deep scratch ran down one side of his face. His eyes fluttered open then closed again.

"Shhhh, it's alright," I choked, stroking his soft hair. The sound of an angry baboon throwing itself against my axe's magical barrier pulled my attention away from my lover. I had a couple of minutes before the shield gave way. I got out my phone and called Aloora. She didn't answer. I speed typed a group text, my eyes darting from my phone screen to the baboon. I sent up a silent prayer that someone would see it. Then I placed myself between Lorandir and the creature and readied myself.

I willed Bloodbane to guide my hands and defeat my foe. I felt the heat of my amethyst pendant against my skin and willed it to give me power over the stone creature. Through the tinted lenses of my goggles, I saw the purple magic of

Avalon flow through my arms and wind around the dwarven axe. I locked my eyes on the baboon just as the magic barrier faded. The creature hadn't expected the shield to disappear and stumbled under the force of its own momentum. I ran forward, taking advantage of its lapse in concentration.

I swung hard. Bloodbane guided my stroke and connected hard with its foreleg. As the blade sunk into the stone, I saw strands of purple magic flow into the creature. For a second, it paused. Then Bloodbane completed its swing and the baboon's leg lay on the ground. The creature stumbled as its limb came away. It jumped to one side and bared its fangs at me. I heard a moan behind me. Lorandir. I turned. The baboon hit me hard in the arm. Its weight forced me to the floor as it gripped me tightly with its legs and tried to sink its jaws into my shoulder. Bloodbane reacted for me. I hacked at the creature desperately.

A dagger appeared at the baboon's ear. It chinked away a shard of stone. The creature didn't seem to notice. Slim hands wrapped around the stone monkey's waist and the pressure on my arm loosened.

Sensing it was being prised free, the baboon clawed at the pale fingers with fury. I heard a gasp of pain that sounded almost musical. One of the hands disappeared from view and reappeared holding another long dagger. Tainted magic flowed through it and blasted a chunk out of the baboon's side. The blast slammed the creature into the ground ten feet away. A strong, slender hand gripped mine and pulled me up. I looked into the pale blue eyes of Espretha.

"Thanks."

The elf maiden shrugged, then adopted a fighting stance, "What the dzrak is that thing?"

I smiled grimly at her use of Dwarfish. Before I had a chance to tell her it was a demon baboon compelled by magic, the creature pounced. It aimed its weighty body at me. Espretha launched her own bolt of magic at the baboon. It sent the avatar careening into the ground with a thud so hard it created a small crater. The baboon jumped up and charged again.

"Why does it want to kill you?"

"No dzraking idea!"

Espretha was right. The creature was wary of Espretha and tried to stay out of the way of her knives and magic, but it kept coming for me. I dodged left to avoid another attack. The monkey raked my neck as it sailed past. It landed, twisted on its three remaining limbs, and charged again. A plan started to form in my mind.

"We need to pin it down!"

Espretha nodded at me like I'd said something perfectly reasonable, "Distract it!"

"Er…"

The agile elf circled around the baboon. Its red eyes flicked from me to her and back again. It pawed the ground as if deciding who the biggest threat was. I shouted and waved my axe. It worked. With a snarl, the large monkey ran towards me, its lopsided gait could have been comical. If a crazy demon baboon with snarling jaws and glowing red eyes could ever be comical.

I hefted Bloodbane and readied myself for the impact. The creature pounced. A scream sounded through the park.

Espretha was there. With a graceful leap, she jumped onto the baboon's back. Its pounce fell short as she forced it to the ground in front of me. It squirmed, but she kept her footing. The thing tried to push itself up. It almost succeeded.

"What now?"

I pulled my thoughts away from wondering just how little the slender elf weighed and instead placed Bloodbane on the back of the creature's head. I leaned my own weight onto the axe haft, keeping the baboon pinned to the ground.

I closed my eyes and willed Avalon's magic through my pendant and onto the axe, praying this would work. The squirming under my axe seemed to lessen.

I risked opening my eyes. Through my goggles, I could see threads of the purple magic fanning out over the stone. They concentrated at the place where my axe connected with the living statue, but they spread fast to cover the entire baboon. As my magic reached out, the tainted blood magic faded until it disappeared entirely. I caught a line of the evil magic retreating into the park. I made to follow it when the screech of tyres brought me back to reality.

Chapter 30

I turned to see Agent Jones running towards me. I checked the stone baboon. The only magic I could sense was the peaceful magic of hope and protection from my pendant mixed with the ancient dwarven power of Bloodbane. Tentatively, I lifted my axe. The baboon stayed still on the floor; it was back to being a lifeless statue.

"Lorandir! He needs help!" I raced over to the stricken elf. I could sense his own healing magic; that familiar sense of bittersweet chocolate, honey mead, and running through a leafy forest that sent my head reeling. It was more subtle than when he healed me. Through my goggles, he glowed softly with the golden green of elven magic. Did that mean he was healing himself? I pushed my crafting goggles up onto my head, knelt beside him and held his hand. I thought I saw his lips curve up in a soft smile at my touch.

"What the dzrak happened here?" Agent Jones loomed over us.

"Someone enchanted that thing so it attacked us."

The shifter looked dubiously at the statue lying in the dry grass. She inhaled deeply. Her eyes narrowed and her hand went to the crossbow in a holster at her thigh. She called for Maxi, her tech expert and marched off.

Espretha joined me beside Lorandir while the Magical Liaison Office searched the area for magic users.

"Thank you," I said. The elf shrugged in response. "How did you even know we were in trouble?"

"Group text. I didn't exactly know what you meant, but I guessed 'Boot Park' meant here," she showed me the garbled text I had sent.

Attacked by lemon balloon in boot park. Loaner hurt. Send help.

Damn autocorrect.

"Will he be alright?"

The elf surveyed her friend, "Healing's not my area of expertise, but I think he'll be OK." She pointed to the deep cut on his face which was already starting to close. I risked lifting up his t-shirt. The fabric was wet with blood and stuck to his skin. Carefully, I eased it away. The bleeding had slowed but the wounds were still open. This was bad. Normally, he could heal anything quickly.

Aloora appeared behind me, "Fascinating. I've heard of healing trances, but this is my first time seeing one." The small gnome handed me a bottle of Madam Mim's Cure All and placed her hand comfortingly on my shoulder before I could growl a reply about her insensitivity to my fiancé possibly dying. I felt tears well up in my eyes and smiled a thank you to her instead. She nodded and walked back to join her team. I tipped some of the thick liquid onto the wounds and then allowed a few drops to fall into Lorandir's mouth. The smell of aniseed, alcohol and herbs hung strongly in the air.

"You might want some of that yourself," Espretha offered, pointing at my neck.

Now she drew my attention to it, I realised I ached from the impact of the stone baboon hitting me and my neck felt raw where it had scraped me. I took a gulp of the Cure All and felt the fiery healing potion flood through me. It tasted awful, but it worked.

Aloora came back over, "Let me drive you to the hospital."

I nodded and squeezed Lorandir's hand again. He stayed unconscious.

Aloora looked from me to the elf then called her superior. Agent Jones picked up the elf easily and carried him to the van. She grunted an order to report to the Magical Liaison Office Headquarters as soon as Lorandir was feeling up to it and then returned to her investigations.

"Take it easy alright, Aloora," I said as I settled Lorandir into a row of seats and tried to lie him down and strap him in. The seatbelts wouldn't cooperate, so in the end I compromised by gripping him tightly as my friend pressed her foot to the accelerator. After we swerved round the first corner, I swore at her and she gave me an apologetic smile.

"Sorry, Dan just likes to be driven fast, don't you?" I stared at the back of her head. Yes, she had started talking to the van. I vaguely remembered Dot naming it Dan the van after I'd imbued it with magic to ward off an attack of hideous ten-legged tarfangtulas. I hadn't realised at the time that my enchantment was permanent. She carried on, "You're really worried about him, aren't you? He'll be OK, you know; elven healing trances are amazing…"

I grunted in acknowledgement as she started on a lecture about something I'd never even heard of before today, "I just want to get him somewhere safe."

"Right," she changed lanes with a cheery wave at the driver of a brown estate car that she'd cut across.

I looked down at the sleeping elf. The deep gash on his face still oozed blood. I could feel the residual aura of his magic and the harsh contrast of the twisted magic that I had sensed during our fight.

Unbidden, my mind went back to when I'd thought I'd lost him during the battle of Avalon. It had felt like my heart had ripped in two. And today felt the same. What if he couldn't recover? What if this trance wasn't strong enough? I blinked back tears, convinced he wasn't going to make it.

Chapter 31

Aloora pulled back into her original lane to a chorus of horns blaring and turned off towards the hospital.

She swerved the van into the drop-off zone while I protested, crushing Lorandir to me and telling him to stay away from any lights. She jumped out and ran into the concrete building.

I stroked Lorandir's forehead and whispered that we were here. He opened bleary eyes, and I supported him out of the van. For a slender elf, he weighed more than I expected as I wrapped one arm around his waist and slowly walked us into the building.

Aloora sprinted back, trailed by two medics who steered a gurney with expert precision. They screeched to a halt next to me and took over, manhandling the elf onto the wheeled bed with practised ease.

One of them spoke to Lorandir while the other peppered me with questions as we raced inside. I'd like to think that the National Health Service would treat everyone equally, but the number of doctors and nurses definitely increased once Aloora mentioned that he was an elven prince.

They ushered us into a private room where a doctor took his blood pressure while a nurse hooked him up to an IV and someone else cut off his clothes before they sterilised and bandaged his wounds. I hung back, watching and shifting from side to side, a thousand questions on my lips.

There was lots of murmuring about elves' healing magic and how that would mix with modern medicine that did not fill me with confidence.

Aloora noticed my concern and elbowed her way into the doctors' conversation, flashing her Magical Liaison Office badge.

I crept from my spot in the corner to Lorandir's bedside and held his hand.

A few minutes later, Aloora joined me.

"They think he's stable."

"Then why isn't he awake?!" I couldn't keep the panic from my voice.

She rubbed my arm, "He's in the best place for care. They're monitoring him closely, but he's not in any pain. He needs time to heal."

I stifled a sob.

"Do you want me to stay?" Aloora's eyes were full of concern.

I shook my head. She pulled me into a hug and slipped me a brand-new bottle of Cure All before letting herself out. Lorandir's eyes flickered, and I moved closer to his side in an instant.

Not knowing what to do, I plumped his pillow, covered him with the pale blue hospital blanked, and then pulled the single chair in the room over to his bed. I perched on the scratchy cushion and let Marco and Mum know where we were. I left out the part about a statue coming to life and attacking us. Texts about the wedding bombarded me. Apparently, the menu was sorted, and they had booked Brinda for a five-hundred-pound deposit. So, it was now imperative we sorted a date.

I looked down at the sleeping elf. "At least you don't have to deal with this," I told him. He mumbled in his sleep. I kissed his forehead and braced myself to call his cousin.

I told Morthimas about the attack and he insisted on coming to the hospital. Less than half an hour later, he threw open the door and marched in. His face blanched when he saw Lorandir on the bed.

He swore in Elvish, "Bloody hell, I've never seen him like this before. Where are the doctors?!"

The King turned around and marched back out. I could hear his musical voice through the walls as he harangued the nearest medical professional. He came back in and sank to his knees next to the bed.

"There's nothing more they can do…"

I nodded, "We just have to wait."

We stayed silent for a long time, until my head drooped forward. The elf tore his gaze from his cousin and took in my dishevelled state, "You should go home, get cleaned up."

I shook my head.

"Go on, you're dead on your feet," his voice softened, "and when he wakes up, he'll want to know you're alright. One of my Councilmembers will escort you. I'll stay right here."

I looked from the King to my fiancé. "You won't leave him?"

"I promise." He shouted an elven name and one of his Council appeared in the doorway. The King explained the plan and the Councillor looked at me.

"Where do you want to go?"

I thought for a moment, "To Lorandir's flat."

The Councilmember nodded and cast a portal in the hospital room. I took a breath and stepped through.

My stomach clenched and dizziness flooded through me. Then we were outside Lorandir's penthouse apartment. I swore and dug around for my key. Typical. But I had my own keys, including the one I had enchanted to open any lock. I concentrated, feeling the magic work on the door. Then we were in.

The Councillor waited outside and took up a guard stance. I ignored him and headed for the shower. Once I was done, I put on one of Lorandir's t-shirts. It covered me like a dress.

I shoved my dirty clothes into the built-in washer dryer and studied the controls. There was no setting for blood or lichen stains. I selected an 'All in One' cycle and hoped that would do it.

I couldn't sleep and I wanted to do something useful. I moved to the tea cupboard and shook my head. My fiancé had an entire cupboard stocked with different teas. Most of them were elven brews with neat flowing script telling anyone who could read Elvish what they were. I couldn't read Elvish.

Instead, I used my phone to search for elven healing teas and then held up the results next to each wooden box. I selected the one that looked most similar to the internet's search and made two cups. The spicy scent of cinnamon filled my nostrils, and I took a sip. It was sweet and spicy. Not bad. For herbal tea.

I screwed the lid tightly on the travel mug. It would be ready for when he woke up. What else? I looked around the kitchen. Chicken soup was meant to be good for ill people, right? I guessed that meant it would be good for Lorandir.

After ninety minutes of chopping, stewing, and stirring, I had made something that resembled soup. It was watery. It had chicken and vegetables in it. I'd even added a chilli pepper after the internet told me that helped people feel better. It made my eyes water, at least that's what I told myself as tears streamed down my face.

I'd caused this. Whatever, whoever was attacking us had been trying to get me and Lorandir, the love of my life had got caught in the crossfire. Was it even fair of me to marry him if I brought him this much pain and suffering?

I decanted the soup into a tub and rubbed my eyes; I wasn't getting any sleep tonight. I had to make sure Lorandir was OK. I headed outside.

"I want to go back to the hospital."

The Councilmember arched one eyebrow, but gathered his power and created another portal. I stepped through, lurching sideways as the nausea hit me again.

Morthimas looked up in surprise, but, even better, Lorandir stirred. His nose twitched then his eyes opened and he pushed himself upright. He winced at the pain from his movement. "What's that smell?"

"Er, chicken soup. I made it for you, to help you feel better," I carried the tub over and set it up on the portable table next to his bed. I studied him carefully and reached out to trace the healing wound on his face with a finger. He shuddered under my touch.

"I'm so sorry," I sobbed.

"Don't even worry about it," he smiled as he said my usual refrain. He picked up a spoon and helped himself to the soup, "You make a wonderful nurse, Amethyst." I blushed. He sniffed again and took a sip. He coughed and forced himself to swallow. "Maybe leave the cooking to someone else though."

I narrowed my eyes and tried a spoonful. I spat it back out instantly, "Ugh, that is awful. Sorry."

He mumbled something and took a long drink of the tea. Then he lay back down, instantly back asleep in his trance. I smiled down at him. No. I loved him too much to leave. Maybe that made me selfish.

I wished I knew who had compelled all these people and now creepy stone statues to attack me. I'd make them pay for hurting my fiancé and then we could get married and dzraking live happily ever after.

Chapter 32

Next morning, I rapped on the non-descript black door of the Magical Liaison Office. The building looked like an ordinary, if old, office building off one of the side streets in Cardiff City Centre. Aloora opened it.

"You'd better come quick, she doesn't like being kept waiting," my friend turned and led the way across the marble floor to the main office without giving us a chance to explain. My boots left wet footprints on the white stone as we walked. Normally, the door to the inner sanctum was closed, but today it was wide open. The enchanted doorknocker looked annoyed as we passed through.

"I don't know why I bother!"

"Shut up, Fred!" Agent Jones boomed from inside. I swallowed nervously. We were late. Apparently, 'as soon as he's feeling up to it' actually meant 'first thing in the morning if he's not in hospital'.

The oversized sofa in his apartment was comfortable and we had fallen asleep. Not even the rain spattering the floor to ceiling windows had woken us. It had taken the sound of my phone blaring out the Superman theme tune to get me up and then the hiss of Aloora's voice asking where we were to propel me to get dressed and out the door in record time.

A flash had almost blinded me just outside the apartment block. It had taken three more flashes for me to realise it was a herd of paparazzi, and they were getting photos of me and Lorandir. And I was in yesterday's clothes. Schiztz.

Lorandir had pulled me back inside the building where a new receptionist with a sour look on her face had batted away the photographers with legalese and ordered us a taxi. She allowed us to use a hidden staff entrance to get out and the driver had raced across the city. My hair was winding its way out of the ponytail I had forced it into. I was already stressed, and I hadn't even had a cup of coffee yet. My hand clenched and unclenched on my axe's handle, a sure sign of nervous energy.

"Come in then!" Agent Jones ordered. My feet obeyed and Lorandir and I walked in and stood on the edge of the oriental carpet in the pentagon shaped room that seemed to host most of the Magical Liaison Office's work. Aloora perched on one of the red leather armchairs. Agent Jones leant against a wall while Maxi fiddled with the huge screen that took up most of another wall. Espretha sat on an office chair with wheels. She was facing the wrong way, so she could use the backrest to lean on while she picked her nails with a thin dagger. Dot emerged from the hidden door that led to the kitchen. The vampire cradled a cup of something in her pale hands. I stared at it hungrily.

"Not coffee," she gave me a wink and lounged on the low Chesterfield sofa facing the screen. Lorandir joined her, matching her lounging pose. I plonked myself in the last remaining seat on the sofa. There was no point trying to match the elegant nonchalance of either the vampire or the elf.

"Right, now we're all here," Agent Jones gave Lorandir and I a sharp glance, "Maxi, you can begin."

"Excellent! Yah, well we've got some totally bizarre readings from the scene yesterday," he pressed a button on his laptop and a graph blazed across the huge wall screen. I stared at the lines. I had no idea what they meant.

"This is the magical signature we got from the wall that housed the statue. And here is the signature on the statue." A new line appeared on the graph. "As you can see, they are totally different, yah?"

We nodded in agreement.

"Espretha explained that you stopped the baboon Amethyst, so I think this reading is your signature." I leant forward, suddenly more interested.

"What are those grey lines at the bottom?"

"That's the low-level magical residue left in the park, mostly by humans, but these spikes are where magical beings interacted with the park."

"Wait, humans have a magical signature?!"

"I mean, it's low level, hardly shows up on the equipment, but yah, everything has a signature. There's a number of theories put forward, personally I favour Henderson's view that…"

Agent Jones coughed pointedly.

"Yah, well, the point is that it matches exactly with the residue of the compulsion magic we found on the goliath in Jarnstradr." A new line traced over the original one on the graph. Maxi carried on excitedly, "And Madam Mim let me run some scans of magical residue left after the Avalon attack to see if there was any lasting damage and, well, look!" Maxi's graph showed another line in bright yellow. This one mapped exactly over the lines from the park and the goliath.

Aloora and the others nodded.

"Er, what does it mean?" I asked stupidly.

"This line was from a scan taken from the library at Avalon."

I frowned. The magical library was the source of Avalon's power for hope and protection. It was also the room where I'd fought Mordred… "It's Mordred's magical signature!"

I stared at Maxi, "Are you trying to tell me that Mordred was here? He was eaten by a dzraking dragon!"

"Apparently not," Agent Jones stepped forward. "Maxi's run the data multiple times and it seems he's alive and here. In Cardiff."

"Schiztz."

"Quite."

"Why is he targeting us?"

Agent Jones gave me a look, "You did try to kill him."

"Yeah, and fair's fair he nearly killed me!"

"Right. Well, I think it's best you keep a low profile and you'll have an agent with you round the clock. Mordred is bad news and who knows what else he's planning. I don't want him running around the city."

"It's going to be hard to keep a low profile with dzraking paparazzi everywhere," I mumbled.

Four pairs of eyes turned to me. Schiztz. I had forgotten about supernatural hearing.

"The wedding's going to have to wait until we catch Mordred. Sorry." It was unlike Agent Jones to apologise for anything and her amber eyes filled with pity. I stared at her. I bristled. My hand clenched Bloodbane subconsciously.

First Mordred tries to destroy Avalon, basically the source of everything good in the world and now, just when things were starting to settle down, he wanted to destroy my wedding. All I wanted was to be with Lorandir and it seemed like I couldn't even make that happen. Lorandir rubbed my shoulder supportively.

"Like dzrak it will," I spoke softly but clearly. Agent Jones stared at me and crossed her arms. I met her gaze steadily. "What if we use the wedding to lure Mordred out? That could work, right? Then we can get rid of him once and for all." I thought I saw something like admiration flicker across her face.

"Can I speak to you for a second?" Lorandir's grip tightened on my shoulder, and he practically propelled me out of the room. The door closed behind us with a click. "You want to use our wedding as a trap for the symbol of everything corrupt?"

"Er," when he put it like that it didn't seem like such a good idea, "I just feel like everything's spiralling away from us. I want to be with you. What happened in the park...it was too close, I could have lost you! And I want our friends to be safe and none of that feels like it can happen if Mordred's out there somewhere, trying to kill us."

I sank against his chest. What had I been thinking? He stroked my hair and then tilted my chin up before brushing his lips against mine in a soft kiss. "Just wanted to be sure."

My heart swelled with love for the elf, and I returned his kiss hungrily. The door knocker did an approximation of a wolf whistle that completely ruined the moment.

"We'd better go back in then."

"What's the magic word?"

"Er, let us in now before I tell Agent Jones on you. Please."

The brass knocker screwed up its ugly face, "No need to be nasty." The door swung open. We stepped through. It shut quickly behind us, the heavy wood smacking my behind as I passed through. I thought I heard muffled sniggering through the door. Cul. I gave the door a quick kick with the back of my boot.

Aloora was waiting just inside while the others pretended to be busy studying books and laptops, "Are you sure about this?"

I looked to Lorandir. He met my brown eyes with his green ones and nodded. "Yep."

As soon as the word was out of my mouth, Agent Jones stepped forward and rubbed her hands together. I wasn't sure I liked the gleam in her eyes. "Right then, let's get started."

Chapter 33

So, it turns out that having the Magical Liaison Office help plan your wedding suddenly made it a lot smoother. Marco practically fainted when I told him we had moved the date up to the following month. He muttered something in Italian that I couldn't understand, but when Agent Jones accompanied him to the company that supplied photo booths, he changed his mind quickly. The shifter arched one eyebrow at the unfortunate sales attendant who tried to say that they didn't have any booths available for the chosen weekend and he volunteered their deluxe package at a discount. I would have laughed, but Jones turned her gaze on me, and I stared down at my shoes instead.

Now I stared at myself in the mirror, waiting to go to, gulp, my wedding. I hadn't ever thought I'd be the sort of girl who would enjoy a big fancy wedding. Dating was so far out of my experience growing up that I hadn't really fantasised about the big day. I certainly couldn't have imagined myself in a custom creation by renowned designer, Madam Tinselle.

I looked at myself in the mirror again. The dress was perfectly proportioned to emphasise my curves in the best possible way. There was a cunning built-in bra system that supported my assets and pushed up my cleavage in the strapless dress. As a nod to winter, a thick fake fur stole was wrapped around my shoulders. Crystals glinted amid the lace and satin as they caught the light. My amethyst pendant hung perfectly centred above the slight dip in the middle of the neckline.

Morthimas had thoughtfully sent a basket of elven beauty products as a present and Espretha had spent an hour helping me with my make up while Aloora wrestled my hair into an intricate half-up do that somehow made me look taller. I heard them join Dot, my third bridesmaid, in the connecting room.

They clinked champagne glasses together and started singing. My lips curled into a smile as I recognised the song. It was the anthem to the hen do that Aloora had thrown me: *Girls Just Wanna Have Fun*. I smiled at my reflection as I thought back to that night.

*****

It had been wet and cold. A typical autumn day in Wales, with the chill in the air reminding us that winter was close. I was at my workbench in Gunther's warehouse, working on protection charms. Since we were using our wedding as a trap, I wanted to make sure all our guests were safe, or as safe as they could be if Mordred attacked. So, I made protection charms as wedding favours. Stupidly, I had decided to make them all in the shape of a tiny dragon, using Errol as my inspiration, and I wanted to make the runes I was enchanting them with to be as subtle as possible.

Obviously, the intricate design took me three times as long as just making plain circular disks, and I wanted to etch our names and the wedding date on the back, too. I leaned back and stretched before ticking off another charm from the list I had created to track my progress. Halfway through and less than a week to go. I reached for the next small sheet of silver I had hammered flat and sketched out the design using the template I'd made to make sure the charms were all the same. I didn't want any infighting over who had got the best wedding favour. There was already going to be enough tension with elves and dwarves in the same room, let alone the added bonus that a dark elf might attack. That's when I heard the noise. Or rather, the lack of noise. Gunther's bustling warehouse had gone silent. I looked up and couldn't see anyone. Odd.

A hand slapped down on my shoulder. I turned and looked up into Gunther's face. He was uncharacteristically serious.

"There's some sort of problem, Amethyst."

I gaped up at him, not understanding. My head reeled. What now? My mind spiralled through all the possibilities: someone was hurt…or dead. I wanted to call Lorandir, but Gunther led me quickly across the vast warehouse to the loading bay. There, all of Gunther's workers were ranged in a large, unnaturally quiet semi-circle. I caught Bethan's smirk. The kobold was enjoying this. That couldn't be good. Pixies, goblins, and an orc were standing next to the five or six kobolds that formed Gunther's current workforce. Gunther pointed at a police officer standing near the doors.

"Ms Amethyst Haernson?"

I nodded, not trusting myself to speak.

"I'm afraid you're under arrest."

"What?" I squeaked. The officer ignored me and took out a pair of handcuffs. He slapped one cuff around my wrist and the other around his own arm. "Why? What have I done?"

"You've been a very bad girl." Dance music boomed around the warehouse and the watching crowd burst into cheers as the police officer began to gyrate. Too slowly, I realised what had happened. I looked around the room and found Aloora and Espretha hiding in Gunther's office. They were laughing so hard, they couldn't stand up straight and Aloora had her dzraking phone out filming my ordeal. I glared at them. I heard a rip to my side and turned back. The 'officer' had just ripped off his shirt revealing a shaved chest. He handed me a bottle of oil and motioned for me to rub it in. I leaned away and shook my head.

"I'll do it!" Bethan leered from the sidelines.

"Be my guest!" I threw the green-skinned kobold the bottle and used my magic to free myself from the metal handcuffs. The 'officer' looked a little put out as the small creature practically ran at him, brandishing the bottle, but he recovered well and allowed her to coat him with the slippery oil.

After more dancing, the stripper pulled off his Velcro-ed trousers to reveal a shiny red thong. He insisted on sitting me down on a chair and giving me the most awkward lap dance ever as I mouthed curses at my so-called best friend and tried not to touch anything. If Aloora ever found the right woman, I vowed I would get revenge for this at her hen do. She was still filming and trying not to laugh as Bethan shoved notes into the back of the stripper's g-string while he thrust his groin at me.

Eventually, the music wound down and the gyrating stopped. The stripper gave a bow and helped me off the chair with a stupid grin plastered over his clean-shaven face.

"That's your lot…but I'm free all afternoon if you want more."

I stared at his naked body, barely covered by the tiny thong in horror. "How much more can there be?" The words were out of my mouth before I could stop them. Fortunately, he laughed and gave me a wink.

Aloora was by my side, "I think that'll be all for now. Thanks Wayne."

Bethan sidled up next to us, "Aww, are you sure we can't bring him along?" She trailed one clawed finger over his abs.

"Alright, back to work everyone!" Gunther shouted, clapping his hands. The distraction allowed Wayne to escape Bethan and grab his fake uniform. "Have a great hen do Ame, and don't worry, I won't tell your Dad."

I gave him a tired smile and picked up my axe and Errol from my workbench. I allowed Aloora to lead me outside before turning on her.

"What were you thinking?"

"That my friend had a sense of humour. Come on, loosen up, it's your last big night of freedom before you tie the knot and I lose you."

She was staring at her sparkly converse shoes, twisting one foot nervously. I pulled her into a hug, "You're not going to lose me."

"Uh, the van's waiting. Can we get a move on before you both start blubbing?" Espretha interrupted. She was standing next to a familiar grey van and holding the door open. I wiped my nose on a piece of tissue paper I found in my jeans' pocket and pulled out my phone.

"Just letting Lorandir know I'll be late getting back."

The others burst into laughter and Aloora clapped me on the back, "Don't worry, he's out on his stag do!"

I tucked away my phone and climbed into the van, wondering what was in store for both of us.

"Welcome to Dan the party van!" Dot practically shouted as I got in. I blinked a couple of times as the vampire shoved a cheap sash over my head and then tried to fix a fake tiara to my hair. I was too distracted to stop her. I stared at the van's transformation. Fluffy pink pom poms covered the webbing on the sides that usually housed weapons and other equipment along with handmade signs proclaiming it was "Amethyst's Hen Do!"

New throws in pink, black and silver replaced the usual colourful crochet blankets. Someone had rigged up a disco ball to the ceiling and it reflected a neon pink glow around the interior. Brinda waved at me from next to the vampire, her pink dress catching the light. I waved back and found a seat.

"Wow, looks great Dot, how long did all this take?"

The vampire beamed at my appreciation, "Not too long, but the penis poms were a bit tricky." She gave me a lewd wink.

Unbidden, my eyes sought out the nearest pom poms. This close I could see that they were hung in pairs. I pulled a pair towards me and let it go quickly. The pom poms were attached to crocheted penises. I tried not to look too closely.

"Cool. How did you get them to look so realistic?" Bethan held one up in the flashing light and studied it carefully.

While Dot started explaining about crochet stitches and wool combinations, Espretha poured me a drink. I sipped the cool prosecco gratefully.

Aloora climbed into the driver's seat and pushed a CD into the built-in stereo system. *Girls Just Wanna Have Fun* blared through the speakers and with a cheer, we were off. Aloora drove us into town and parked the party van in the Magical Liaison Office's underground car park. Errol snagged one of the crocheted phalluses and insisted on chewing it as he took his place draped across my shoulders.

"Won't Jones mind?" I whispered as we crept up the spiral staircase that led to the ground floor.

"Won't Jones mind what?"

I jumped as the shifter's voice boomed from the top of the stairs. Errol dug his claws into my shoulders and dropped his chew toy at her voice.

"Er…" I looked around guiltily. It hadn't been my idea to come here but the sash draped across my body proclaimed I was the hen.

"Just joking! Now come on or we'll be late!" Agent Jones clapped me on the back, then bent to pick up the knitted creation that Errol had dropped. The shifter studied it for a second before handing it back to the small wyrm. "Nice penis."

I felt my cheeks heat, but Dot answered, "Thanks! It took a bit of experimenting to get the head right."

Agent Jones headed for the door. She was in a cream suit with a blush-coloured shirt that sank into a deep v under her practical yet stylish raincoat. I guess that was her way of dressing up for a night out. I looked down at my own shabby clothes. My old t-shirt and jeans were great for work, but not for a night on the town. I mentioned this to Aloora, and she slapped her hand to her forehead before rushing back down the stairs.

The silence was a little uncomfortable while we waited for her to return. I used the time to finish my second glass of fizzy wine. After an age, Aloora reappeared waving a carrier bag full of clothes.

"Got this from your room," she said as she shoved the bag into my arms, pointed me to the toilets and told me to get changed. I got dressed as fast as I could, considering I got stuck in the sash and the tiara was caught in a tangle of my hair. I tried to free the plastic crown, but it was wedged in. I gave up and emerged wearing a burgundy-coloured steampunk style corset top and a clean pair of dark indigo denim jeans. I kept on my gothic style leather boots and my red leather jacket.

The hens all gave a cheer as I emerged from the bathroom. I noticed Espretha discreetly push an empty wine bottle behind a large potted plant in the hallway. Then we were out in the cold streets of Cardiff.

Chapter 34

Aloora led the way along the high street and towards the main drinking street. The sun had already set, but it was still early and not many people were out and about in the heavy rain. Once we were on St Mary Street, the ladies propelled me towards a cocktail bar with a discreet white five-pointed star on a black sign.

As the sign swung in the wind, I noticed the metallic red droplet in the middle of the star. We went straight in, and the hostess led us to the bar. We were the only people here. I ran my hands along the burnished surface appreciatively. It was made from sheets of copper hammered together and reflected the antique style bulbs, giving the large room a cosy, warm feel. There were red velvet curtains trimmed with gold draped across the walls that should have looked tacky but instead added an old-world glamour to the room.

A bartender in a tight black top took up position behind the bar and welcomed us to the Blud Alchemy Cocktail Making Experience. He introduced himself as Steve and I did a double take as his wide smile revealed pointed fangs. We were in a vampire bar. I looked at the others surreptitiously. No one else was worried and Dot gave me a thumbs up. I guess that meant we were safe here. Steve carried on with the introduction. We were going to make three cocktails. First up was something called Witches' Brew.

Steve demonstrated how to make the concoction before handing out cut glass tumblers in the shape of cauldrons to each of us. We poured in the vodka, lime juice, lemonade, and absinthe before Steve put in a tiny amount of dry ice to create a smoking effect. The drinks looked amazing, and we clinked our cauldrons together.

"Cheers!" I took a sip. It was strong, but the lemonade and lime flavours balanced out the aniseed taste of the absinthe, meaning it was a warming aftertaste instead of a full-on kick in the mouth.

Bethan gave me a wink before pouring another shot of absinthe in her glass. Steve caught her and moved the bottles of alcohol out of her reach with vampiric speed.

Steve handed us a menu and said I could choose the next drink we would make. My eyes scanned down the list. All the drinks had supernatural names: the Zombie, the Ghostly Spirit, After Midnight, the Witching Hour and so on.

"How about the Bloody Bellini?"

"I love that one!" Dot clapped her hands together, "I'll have the original please Steve."

I looked back at the menu. I hadn't even clocked the vampire original variant underneath. It came with actual blood. Steve laughed and showed us how to crush raspberries with sugar to make a thick syrup. He poured his own syrup into the glass so that some of it looked like blood dripping down the side. We tried to copy him. My syrup wasn't thick enough and ran down my glass and onto the copper counter. Steve uncorked a bottle of champagne with a flourish and topped off our Bellinis before garnishing them with a fake set of sugary vampire fangs. We chinked our glasses together and tried the drinks.

"Delicious!" proclaimed Aloora.

Dot's eyes turned a brighter shade of red as she drank her version down. Steve had given her own version of the syrup, which looked like it contained real blood. She finished her Bellini quickly and her eyes dulled to their usual darker red. She licked her lips and looked a little embarrassed.

"So, are you going to tell us how you and Lorandir got together?"

I chewed on the sweet vampire fangs and thought, "Well we sort of got together after the Equinox Ball…but our first kiss was before that."

"I love first kiss stories. Tell us," the vampire demanded. I tried to protest, but the other women echoed Dot's request, except for Agent Jones; she kept her eyes on her drink.

"Er, OK, well, it was after the dragon awoke and destroyed a chunk of Cardiff Castle. I passed out and when I woke up, Lorandir was there and then…we kissed."

"That's it?!" Bethan shrieked. The small kobold was already looking worse for wear.

Aloora rolled her eyes at me and Espretha made a strange expression as Dot begged for more details, "So romantic, just like sleeping beauty. What was it like?"

"It was the best kiss of my life." I finished my Bellini and licked the spilt juice off my fingers.

Dot clutched her hands to her heart. I had no idea she was such a romantic.

"And your final cocktail tonight is: 'Til Death Do Us Part," Steve interrupted. I thought about my plan to use the wedding as bait for Mordred. 'Til Death Do Us Part sounded about right.

Again, the vampire demonstrated how to mix the drink with panache boarding on showing off as he flipped metal tumblers into the air and caught blocks of ice behind his back. He offered us the opportunity to throw our cocktail mixers up and catch it one at a time.

Espretha, Dot and Agent Jones all threw theirs high over the bar and caught the mixer with ease. Agent Jones even got it to somersault three times in the air to cheers from the rest of us. Aloora managed one somersault and caught the metal tumbler with both hands. Brinda threw the mixer gently straight up and down, catching it easily. Bethan contented herself with a shake of hers before pouring it into the waiting glass. I threw it and fumbled the catch. Watermelon juice and vodka went everywhere.

"Not a problem," Steve's grin looked forced, but he wiped up the mess, remade my cocktail and then poured out two shots. "One for the winner," he pushed the shot glass to Agent Jones, "and for the bride." He slid the second glass to me. I downed it and felt the vodka warm my throat.

He lined up the bright red cocktails in front of us. Steve took a long-handled match from behind the bar and lit it. Errol's nostrils began to smoke. Schiztz. I had an idea where this was going. Before Steve could light the cocktails, my wyrm breathed fire across the copper countertop, setting the drinks ablaze. Everyone stared. Then they started clapping. Errol gave a small snort of satisfaction before he settled back down on my shoulder.

I blew out the flames and tried the bright red cocktail. It was sweet and refreshing with a smoky aftertaste thanks to the fire. Steve leant across and topped it up with the remains of the champagne bottle. The small bubbles made me sneeze. To his credit, Steve ignored me while I grabbed for a napkin.

"And now ladies, that is the end of the Blud Alchemy Cocktail Experience, please enjoy the rest of your night."

We stayed for one more round and I thanked my hens for arranging a unique experience. Dot shrugged easily, causing her sparkly knitted sweater dress to shimmer in the soft lighting, "It was nothing. The owner owed me a favour and besides, this isn't all we've got in store for you."

"What does that mean?" I looked at each of them, but they were poker faced.

Aloora checked her watch, "Time to go."

Bethan drained the dregs of her drink and licked the sugar-coated rim as if she was trying to eke out every bit of alcohol. She swayed towards the door and into Agent Jones. The shifter didn't look happy, but she supported the small kobold into the night air and kept her upright as we crossed back towards the castle.

I recognised our next destination. Aloora had booked a table at the Rummer. I ordered the steak and chips without thinking, along with some water. I needed something to counteract all the alcohol I'd just consumed. Unperturbed, Espretha ordered wine for the table and poured each of us a large glass.

"To true love!" she proclaimed without looking at me, then she downed her drink. Not to be outdone, Bethan finished her glass as well and poured another. A sheen appeared over the kobold's yellow eyes; she didn't look too good.

The food arrived quickly, and we ate more quietly. I had a strong constitution thanks to my dwarven blood, but the others were less able to process the strong drinks and the food definitely helped. Even Aloora, the health-conscious gnome, had opted for complex carbs to help absorb the booze. I saw Brinda discreetly move her wine away and pour herself another glass of water.

I insisted on having dessert. The chocolate fudge cake here was too good to pass up, almost as good as Brinda's brownies. Dot insisted we swap places in between courses so we could get to know each other better.

Espretha squeezed into the seat next to mine while the waiter brought over the slices of cake. They arrived steaming hot with warm chocolate sauce oozing over the rich sponge. I tucked in. The elf toyed with her food, moving the creamy vanilla ice cream into the hot sauce and watching it melt. I eyed it too, wondering if she was going to eat it and how greedy it would be to ask to have it. After all, it was my hen do. She interrupted my gluttonous thoughts.

Espretha stared at her dessert and took another drink of wine, "I do wish you well, you know."

"Er, OK...thanks. Are you sure you're OK?"

"Me? I'm fine. I mean, did I think we might end up together once? Yes. And was he my closest childhood friend? Yes. But it makes sense, you and Lorandir. It's almost like fate, something out of a fairy tale…an elf and a half-dwarf. Of course, he had to choose you." Her voice was heavy with sarcasm.

I chewed slowly. I had no idea what to say.

She sighed, "You make him happy, and I am glad for him." She sounded almost convincing. "I'll tell you this though, if you hurt him in any way, I will kill you." I felt something sharp poke into my stomach and looked down. She had a knife in her hand. I swallowed the piece of cake in my mouth.

"I promise you I'm not going to do anything to hurt him."

"You'd better not, or…" she dug the blade a little further into my corset top. Errol hissed at her.

"Is everything alright over there?" Agent Jones frowned in our direction.

Espretha settled herself back, the knife gone from sight.

"Er, yep, yeah we're all fine." I finished my chocolate fudge cake in silence.

Back in the chilly night air, Aloora announced our final destination, "To the Goat!"

I frowned. The olde worlde supernatural pub didn't exactly seem like a prime hen do destination. I was about to object when Bethan collapsed onto the pavement.

"I knew she'd drunk too much!"

"I'm fine! My legs just don't seem to be able to go forward…" the scrawny kobold tried to stand. And fell over again.

"I think maybe you should call it a night."

"I'm perfectly fine," she slurred. She pulled herself upright before tottering over to a wall. She vomited loudly and vociferously. "I think maybe I should get a cab."

"I'll take her home," Brinda offered in her soft voice.

"Are you sure?"

The café owner nodded, "I've got an early start tomorrow and it's a match day so it's going to be extra busy in the café. I'll see you soon."

We sheltered from the rain in a doorway with them until they were safely in a registered taxi and told Brinda to call us when she got in. You couldn't be too careful. Then we headed to the Tudor ambiance of the Goat. The pub touted itself as the oldest supernatural pub in Cardiff, and it was easy to believe. With its wonky black beams and fake flickering candles in metal sconces, it certainly looked the part.

We were in the middle of a game of 'Never have I ever…' and I had learned more than I ever wanted to know about Agent Jones' sex life, when Goat stepped out from behind the bar and moved to the heavy wooden door. He drew the thick iron bolts across with ease and grinned at the bar, showing long yellow teeth.

"Welcome to the Saturday Night Lock In!" he boomed.

The punters around us burst into cheers and started moving tables against the walls. I stared, completely forgetting our game. I turned back to see my hen party donning pink Stetson hats and laughing. Dot shoved one over my tiara. What the dzrak was going on?

Goat moved to a microphone at the far end of the room and donned his own cowboy hat, "Welcome fair patrons to our monthly line dancing lock in! It's dance till you drop and drink when you drop out!"

Aloora dragged me onto the newly cleared dance floor where everyone had arranged themselves into lines and were looking expectantly at the area that might generously be called a stage.

"What the dzrak? I thought the Goat's lock ins were salacious orgies or something?"

A werewolf behind me chuckled, "That's the last Friday of the month, if you're interested."

I gave a weak smile and turned back to my friends. A goblin in a white cowboy hat with matching boots grabbed the mic and pressed play on a boombox. Country music blared across the bar and the small goblin started do-si-doing while calling out moves to the customers. I tried to join in but it was clear that many of the others were regulars or semi-professionals.

When the goblin compere found out I was a bride to be, she dragged me up for a dance off with Goat himself. He won. Obviously. I was about as coordinated as a duck with two left feet.

But he was a good sport and gave us all a round of strong dwarven ale as a runner-up prize. It was past two in the morning when I arrived back at Lorandir's flat. Errol took himself straight to bed without even eating any coal. It had been a long night for the little wyrm. I yawned and heard a strange sound from the bathroom. I placed one hand on Bane and knocked lightly on the door.

"Lorandir?"

The elf opened the door. His eyes were a glassy green and he seemed to be having trouble focusing. "Amethyst!" he lurched forward, "Did you have fun at the hen do?"

I helped him to the large sofa and laughed, "Are you drunk?"

He considered his answer and put a long finger to his lips, "Maybe," he frowned, "how many units are in a yard of mead?"

I hadn't ever seen my husband-to-be drunk before. I patted his hand and went to get a glass of water. "This will help. Drink it all before you go to sleep. So, how was your stag do then?"

The elf nodded, then stared at the tiara still stuck in my hair. He raised one hand up to my curly hair, "You look like a princess." He smiled, closed his eyes and fell back against the sofa. I cried out in concern, but he started snoring. I pulled a blanket over him and went to our bedroom to let him sleep it off.

***

Unconsciously, my hand reached up to pat one of the twists in my hair. Today I really did look like some sort of princess. I stopped myself from touching my curls just in time. My hair was unruly at the best of times; it didn't need any help messing up the elegant do. A soft knock sounded on the bedroom door before it was pushed open. Aloora's head appeared.

"Are you ready?"

I picked up Bloodbane from where I had left it on the hotel bed. I had been clear; no weapons, no wedding. Madam Tinselle hadn't been thoughtful enough to include a holster with my outfit, but the elves had turned the axe into the most massive, fragrant bouquet by covering the blade with deep red roses, lilies and other small star-shaped flowers I didn't know the names of. The glowing runes gave the bouquet an ethereal shine and illuminated the star flowers. My axe in my hand, I met my chocolate brown eyes in the mirror. I nodded to myself, then turned to my friend. It was time to go.

Chapter 35

The upmarket hotel was a short walk from the castle, but, being a bride, I couldn't possibly walk there. Instead, two vintage cars waited outside to take me and my bridesmaids to the wedding. The cream coloured 1930s style Rolls-Royces were gorgeous. Lorandir had chosen them, saying they reminded him of the first car he had ever seen. I had blinked at the sudden reminder of just how old he was, but was happy he had decided something.

Marco had nearly driven me mad with options for invitation fonts and chair back colours. I had never had to make so many decisions about things that I had never known existed, let alone were important. After Marco had gaped at my original choice of font – Times New Roman, don't judge me, I wanted to keep things simple and readable – I had come up with a decision-making technique.

Basically, I asked Marco's opinion first and went with whichever option he preferred. It meant we had unreadable invites in some fancy gothic calligraphy, but I was spared his disapproving frowns.

I took a deep breath. The decision making was over. All I had to do was get to the venue, not to get killed by my dark elf stalker and marry the man of my dreams. How hard could that be?

I moved out of the revolving doors of the hotel and was immediately blinded by the bulbs of many cameras. One of the downsides to my plan was that we had to announce our wedding date and location as publicly as possible to make sure that Mordred knew about it.

It was a great exclusive for Aloora's social media channels, and it had caused a slew of headlines. And worst of all, it meant I was now wading through a sea of paparazzi anxious to get a shot of the half-dwarf commoner marrying an elven prince. That was the story the press was going for anyway. I tried to smile and silently thanked Madame Tinselle for her creation; there was no way I was going to accidentally flash someone in this dress.

One of them asked when the baby was due, and I smiled broadly and stamped on his foot as I made my way to the car. I got past them without swearing out loud and stood at the door of the rear car as a driver in dove grey livery held it open for me. How the dzrak was I meant to get in there?

I surrendered my axe bouquet to Espretha while I climbed in and scooted across the leather seats. Aloora bundled the tiers of my dress in behind me. The creamy white fabric took up almost the entire back seat, but she managed to get me in. Espretha handed me back the oversized bouquet and the driver shut the door. We were ready.

The bridesmaids climbed into the front Rolls-Royce with ease. I thought I heard Aloora asking about horsepower. The engines purred to life.

The driver turned into the Saturday afternoon traffic. Once we were out of sight of the press, the driver pulled into an alleyway. The other Rolls was already waiting for us, along with the Magical Liaison Office van. I got out of the car without ripping my dress and grabbed my axe bouquet. Agent Jones leant against the van, tapping one foot impatiently.

"Running late?"

"It's a bride's prerogative," I replied.

She nodded and took my place in the fancy vintage car. She wore a wig made to look like my hair and a cream suit, so anyone looking into the car would see white clothes and think it was me. We were banking on Mordred attacking the bride at the entrance to the castle. If he waited until I was inside, Agent Jones had a dozen agents posing as guests and staff ready for him.

And now, if he attacked the car, he'd have an angry, armed Agent Jones to deal with plus the driver who was another MLO agent.

Aloora got out of the front car and helped manoeuvre me into the van. It was a lot easier getting in through sliding side doors and I didn't have to worry so much about crumpling my skirt. I made myself comfortable on the seats. Someone, I guessed Dot, had strung lacy bunting around the interior and covered the chairs with white blankets to give it a bridal feel. I smiled at the young agent stuck driving me to the wedding.

He was wearing the same uniform as the other drivers, and he looked excited to be on the mission. He grinned back.

"Ready?" he asked, bouncing in his seat.

I nodded. He spoke into a walkie talkie and confirmed everyone else was ready before following the two vintage cars out into the traffic…and almost immediately stopping. The cars inched forward as early Christmas shoppers crossed the road in front of the near stationary traffic. Minutes rolled by and we had barely moved.

Another ten minutes passed, and we were at another set of traffic lights. I played with my necklace absentmindedly as I tried not to think too hard. I looked out of the tinted window at a group of shoppers heaving paper bags into the bus. One of the bags split and a biscuit tin rolled into the road. I looked at the clock in the car.

We had been in the same queue of traffic for thirty minutes. It was one thing for a bride to be fashionably late, but this was another level.

"Don't worry, I know a short cut," the driver turned off. The other cars stayed in the traffic jam, inching forward. I craned my neck looking out of the window to see the others.

"Shouldn't we tell them to come this way too?"

The driver stayed silent as he took us down a road with fewer cars. A bad feeling crept up my spine. I reached for my phone instinctively before remembering I had given it to Aloora for safe keeping. She was allowed a small clutch bag with her bridesmaid outfit. I was only allowed a bouquet. At least it was a bouquet slash axe. I rested one hand on the handle for reassurance.

"Er, I really think we should wait for the other car. They're meant to arrive before me."

"Oh, I've waited long enough," the driver's voice was angry and hard.

Schiztz. I felt the insidious tainted magic that I had come to associate with the dark elf. This wasn't part of the plan.

"Mordred?"

The driver laughed unnaturally. Not Mordred then. But someone he was compelling. If I could break the enchantment, maybe I could get things back on track. I tried pressing Bloodbane to the driver's grey hair. Flowers covered the blade, and I couldn't get the metal to touch his skin. Abruptly, the van pulled to a stop outside a cemetery.

I fell back against the seat and scrambled to my feet. The driver had already got out of the van and opened the door for me. I sorted through the options in my mind.

Part of me wanted to stay inside, cowering. A scream sounded from behind the iron railings. Dzrak it. I couldn't let someone else get hurt because of this dzraker. I made my choice and shuffled out of the van, clutching the oversized bouquet like it was some sort of talisman. It wasn't a dignified exit and the driver stood waiting patiently, an eerie red glow in his eyes.

I thanked him automatically and watched as he shut the door, got back into the front seat and sat waiting. Not weird at all. I took a deep breath and moved towards the cemetery gates.

Chapter 36

The dark elf couldn't have picked a more appropriate setting to kill me. Gothic Victorian monuments to death towered over me as I picked my way along the gravel path. A crow cawed and flew across my path to perch in a gnarled yew tree, thick with waxy red berries. I recognised the scream-like sound that had convinced me to leave the van. Dzraking hell, I was an idiot.

A flock of the noisy birds followed it and the branches bent with the weight of the corvids. My treacherous mind threw up a thought that crows hung around battlefields waiting for dead bodies. Schiztz. I glared at the birds and kept going. I was not going to die today.

I held the bouquet like the weapon it was and moved forward. A high-pitched laugh echoed around the graveyard. I turned, waving the bouquet. My dress swished around me elegantly, like I was at a dance.

"I'm here Mordred. Come out and face me!" More laughter. "Unless you're scared, you spineless piece of schiztz."

This time, the dark elf stepped from behind a huge tomb with a statue of a weeping angel perched on top of it. He leant against the mossy stone and studied his fingernails. He wore a ragged tunic and trousers that hugged his legs so tightly they looked like they might be cutting off the circulation to his feet. His hair was unkempt, reflecting the wild look in his dark eyes. Most of his face was covered by bubbling yellow scar tissue.

The sting of his tainted magic rolled off him and made me involuntarily back up a step. I wrinkled my nose. It wasn't just the magic. He stank. A thick stench of brimstone, dirt, and sweat clung to him. Finally, he looked me up and down appreciatively, his eyes lingering on my cleavage.

"Well, well, you are a pretty thing when you make an effort, aren't you? It almost makes me sorry I'm going to kill you, unless…have you come to offer yourself to me?"

"You wish! I want to get back to my wedding. The wedding you abducted me from…"

The dark elf interrupted me, "Yes, it's poetic, isn't it? You stole my dream of Avalon from me, so I will steal your dream of love from you."

I took up a fighting stance underneath the voluminous dress. He didn't notice. A crow flew in front of his face. With an absent-minded flick of his wrist, the bird collapsed in on itself before falling to the ground. I swallowed down the bile that crept into my throat. I had to distract him. I kept him talking, playing for time and praying that I could get out of this alive. I swallowed again, "I thought the dragon ate you, how did you escape?"

A frown played across his grey face, "The beast did consume me. I don't know how you did it, my own mount turned traitor... Through the agony of the dragon's stomach acids," here, he touched his scarred face unthinkingly, "I conjured a portal and escaped. It has taken me time to regain my strength, but I will kill you and then I will find your lover and kill him and then I will find…"

"Got it. You'll find everyone I love and kill them all. Classic bad guy, I mean it's not original, but hey, strong delivery."

"You will regret your insolence! What does that elf even see in a half-breed like you? He must be deluded. Unless…are you with child?"

I was too shocked to even swear. Instead, my body reacted. I ran towards the dark elf, hefting my large axe above my head. I was done with everyone judging our relationship and I was done with everyone thinking I was pregnant!

He smiled. Magic crackled along his fingers and snapped in an arc towards me. I spun to the side. The smell of burning fabric filled my nostrils. I glanced down, breaking my momentum. The hem of my wedding dress now sported a large burn mark.

"You cul! You'll pay for that!"

Another bolt of magic sparked towards me. I dived behind a large gravestone; the lichen leaving yellow and green stains on the creamy dress. Mordred laughed. I felt the tang of more tainted magic being gathered and braced myself. A split second before the gravestone exploded, I sprinted behind a huge Celtic style cross. I heard the beautiful dress tear as it caught on a branch. Sirens sounded outside the cemetery. My heart fluttered with hope that backup had arrived. I just had to keep him busy and dodge his magic. I risked peeking out from behind my hiding place. Mordred frowned in the direction of the road. He had heard the sirens too.

"You are unarmed, small dwarf. Let us not prolong this charade anymore. I'm feeling generous so, if you come out now, I shall spare your loved ones. It's you I want anyway. I will even make your death quick."

I stepped out, one hand held up and the other clutching my flowers. "How about a fair fight? No magic."

The dark elf laughed again, "You think you can beat me? Then so be it!"

"Let's do this," I switched my grip on the flowers and flicked my hair out of my face. He screwed up his face as he took in my two-handed grip on the bouquet.

"You would fight me with flowers?"

"I'm a bride. You expect me to carry a weapon on my wedding day?"

He laughed again. It was a horrible reedy sound, like he didn't have much practice laughing, "Oh, this will be good."

He rushed towards me with supernatural speed. I caught the crackle of magic before I saw it. Lying cul. I muttered the Dwarfish word for shield, and Bloodbane responded with an invisible barrier. The blast of magic crashed into the shield. The force of it pushed me backwards onto the mound of an old grave. I mumbled an apology to the dead occupant. I had a few minutes before the shield collapsed. I moved forward, pushing Mordred backwards. He let off a couple more blasts at the shield before drawing his sword.

I gritted my teeth and forced my will into Bloodbane to maintain the barrier for as long as I could. The dark elf attacked ferociously, spittle flying from his mouth in rage as he tried to strike me. I felt the shield falter. Dzrak it, I'd thought I had more time. I'd have one shot to make this count. I readied myself, shifting my grip on the axe bouquet. I waited, judging my timing.

Mordred lifted his arm and struck again. I willed the barrier to drop. The dark elf expected his blade to meet the invisible shield, instead the full force of his blow carried through to the floor. His eyes widened in shock as he overbalanced. I stepped forward and brought my axe down hard. He twisted so the blade connected with his shoulder instead of his neck. A flurry of blossoms exploded with the impact, sending a sweet scent into the air.

He batted away the rose petals with his good arm and turned to face me. One arm hung limply at his side. Hatred lit up his eyes.

"You will not defeat me!"

The dark elf lunged towards me. Two crossbow bolts twanged at him. I looked up and caught sight of one of Maxi's drones flying overhead. Mordred twisted mid-leap and avoided them in some sort of move that looked like it belonged in the Matrix. He landed on his feet, hissed at me and ran towards a large crypt. He blasted the door open and sprinted inside, away from the drone.

Chapter 37

I pushed myself up and looked at the drone. It had the name 'Tyrone' written on it in neat, black letters. "You know, I could really use some backup here!"

It might have been my imagination, but I thought a light on its metal body flashed off and on. Was it winking at me?

I shook my head and focused. I felt my amethyst pendant heat on my neck. Channelling all the positivity, hope and love in the stone's magic towards my axe, I sent a silent message to Bloodbane; let me live. The axe guided my feet. I walked to the crypt.

"Enough Mordred," I tried again, "Give yourself up."

A bolt of magic thudded into the stone by my head and gave me my answer. I weighed up my advantages; I had my axe. Good. I'd made him angry. Not so good. And now he was panicked and hiding in a crypt. Really not good. Holding Bloodbane in front of me, I took a step forward.

The drone swooped down in front of me and headed into the darkness. I saw the red flashes as Mordred aimed his magic at the electronic device.

Using the distraction, I ran down the stone steps, brandishing Bloodbane in front of me. My eyes adjusted to the light quickly, thanks to my dwarven dark vision. Mouldy air crowded into my lungs, and I told myself that I would not throw up.

Mordred launched another bolt at the ceiling where the drone hovered, dodging that way and this. I crept behind one of three tombs in the dank crypt and edged forward.

A loud crack reverberated through the underground space, followed by a crash as the drone went down. Mordred laughed his hideous high-pitched snigger and stepped over to the flailing drone. He lifted his sword.

I hefted Bloodbane and charged from my hiding spot, trusting the ancient weapon to help me. He turned, his supernatural hearing picking up my footprints on the damp floor.

I dodged his first blow and heard his blade connect with the wall. He recovered quickly and came at me again. I wasn't fast enough to avoid his next swipe, and hot blood flowed from my arm. I winced at the impact and backed away, waving Bloodbane wildly.

Eery shadows caught his face in the strange half-light of the underground tomb. He grinned, showing yellowing teeth. He lunged. I twisted to one side, hitting a wall in my desperation. I backed along the rough stone, trying to keep out of reach of his blade, desperately blocking blows with my axe. Then I found myself in a corner.

I swung wildly at him, forcing my way out of the damp corner. He parried my blow with ease and brought his sword under my reach. I heard more fabric rip as his sword tore through my dress and found my flesh. I gasped at the sharp burst of pain. His sword stuck in the folds of material, keeping him close to me.

He snarled and gripped my neck with his free hand. I clawed at him and hit him awkwardly with the haft of my axe, but his grip tightened. He pushed me back until my back pressed against the cold, mossy wall of the chamber.

Anger like I had never known surged through me. I was not going to die on my dzraking wedding day! I grabbed his wrist, using my strength to break his grip. I couldn't even budge him. My vision blurred. A crazy thought popped into my mind. Instead of fighting, I could let him think he'd won.

I relaxed, allowing my eyes to flutter closed. A look of triumph crossed his face. I kicked up and felt my boot connect with his groin.

He grunted in pain and his grip loosened. I planted my feet, snaked one hand behind his head and twisted, yanking him forward to headbutt him before he could recover. I let him go and shook my head, trying to get rid of the stars that swam across my vision.

I tried not to worry about having a concussion and focused on the elf. He staggered back, swaying slightly but he had wrenched his sword free of my dress.

I stumbled forward while he was off balance and thwacked the flat of my axe against his head. Hard. He wobbled but stayed upright. I twisted my grip, but he moved backwards, avoiding my next swipe. On the attack again, he came at me. I sidestepped Mordred's lunge, blocking it more easily now he was dazed. I hooked one of the double axe heads around his blade and tugged it free from his hand. It fell to the ground with a thud.

"Give it up, Mordred," I rasped.

"Hah!"

I felt him gather his magic to his hands. I wanted to dive behind a tomb, but Bloodbane reacted before I could think. My feet moved forward. I cried out; something between a war cry and a shriek of terror. The axe's fire rune activated without me saying anything. I raised it up as the evil magic blossomed in his palms.

With a fleshy thud, I cleaved his hand from his body in a flurry of blossoms. The dark elf's magic died on his fingertips. He screamed and cursed. The charred smell of burnt flesh filled the stale air of the crypt. I felt the axe baying for more.

Mordred rolled around on the floor, cradling the stump on the end of his arm. It would be so easy to end him now. I stepped forward; axe raised.

A net fell from the ceiling. I could sense the magic dampening enchantment woven into it. I looked up at the low-flying drone hovering above us.

He shook his head, "I will not be a prisoner again!"

Maxi's voice sounded through the drone's speaker system, "A containment team is on the way. Amethyst, get outside; your ride is waiting."

I looked again at Mordred, still struggling against the net. Footsteps sounded aboveground and then four agents pounded down into the crypt, their weapons trained on the dark elf. I lowered Bloodbane and climbed the steps back up to the cemetery slowly, my body aching at the exertion. The sky was bright after my brief time underground, and I had to blink a few times to make sense of what I saw. A sapphire blue dragon lay in the graveyard, staring at me with bright yellow eyes. Aloora shouted down from its back.

"Thought you might want a ride to the castle."

I nodded dumbly and handed her my axe. A handful of red and white flowers still clung to it. I climbed up to join her on its back. "Are you sure this is a good…" I didn't get any further. She gargled something in Draconic and the dragon launched itself into the air. I put all my energy into gripping onto her, screwing my eyes shut and not throwing up. This was a bad idea. Several lifetimes later, a thud announced our landing in the grounds of Cardiff Castle. Aloora assured me we had been in the air for two minutes.

Lorandir waited for me to slide down. He took me by the elbow and led me off to one side. I was suddenly cold and shaking. He rubbed my bare arms, healing my wounds with his familiar magic, and then hugged me tightly.

"Isn't it bad luck for us to see each other before the wedding?" I asked quietly.

"I think we've had enough bad luck today to last us a lifetime," he pushed me away and met my eyes, "Will you marry me, Amethyst Haernson?"

I reached up to pat my hair, which had fallen from its elegant twist, and looked down at my torn, blood-stained dress. Then I met Lorandir's green eyes. My fiancé was looking at me like I was the most gorgeous woman in the world. Dzrak it. This look was more 'me' anyway. I smiled up at him.

"Of course I will."

Lorandir extended his arm, and I slipped my hand into the crook of his elbow.

Chapter 38

Marco insisted I still had to enter the 'proper way'. A red carpet had been laid across the wooden bridge over the dry moat. Marco claimed it gave an 'Oscar experience'.

Squelching along the luxurious, but damp, carpet – thank you Welsh weather – hand in hand with my gorgeous elf, I was glad my friend had ignored my protestations and stuck with his 'wedding vision'.

Our guests lined the bridge and cheered, celebrating our happiness. Dad's smile looked a little forced and Lorandir's mum looked more like she was scowling, but her teeth were showing, and she was clapping. A gaggle of paparazzi snapped pictures. I didn't even care what the headlines would be; they weren't allowed past the castle's moat, and they weren't going to ruin our day.

We paused for a photo with our official photographer as our guests made their way inside for the ceremony. Maxi snapped happily from behind a huge camera lens and then insisted on getting drone shots from every conceivable angle. Finally, we made our way towards the great hall. I let go of Lorandir's hand and allowed him to enter first. Dad was waiting for me at the large, newly refurbished doorway. A tear glistened in his eye as he pulled me towards him.

"You look beautiful, love. Now are you sure he's the one for you?"

I kissed his cheek and clasped his forearm, "I'm sure Dad. I've made my choice."

He nodded and rearranged his oiled beard, so it sat neatly against the smart grey suit jacket. The grey set off the coloured family tartan of his kilt perfectly and he offered me his arm. As we walked into the hall, I heard Marco mutter into a walkie talkie, "Go petals."

Aloora and Espretha appeared inside the doorway and walked side by side down the aisle in the strangest pairing of bridesmaids I'd seen; a five-foot nothing gnome next to a willowy elf. Both wore deep burgundy red gowns that hugged their figures.

Deep red rose petals fell as if carried by a gentle breeze down from displays magically suspended above another red carpet. I sensed the elven magic at work. I took a breath and stepped through the door.

An underground cellar had been restored and transformed into a magical setting. Soft electric torches lined the room and spotlights in the apex of the vaulted ceiling threw atmospheric shadows across the stone walls. Tapestries hung either side of a wooden door depicting a small dragon that looked a lot like Errol.

I looked to the end of the aisle, past the seated guests who were gazing at me with love, pride and, in the case of Lorandir's Mum, a hint of disbelief. Lorandir was facing the stone wall. I watched as Morthimas nudged him and the elf turned. His face lit up with love as he saw me, and a huge smile crept across his face. It was worth almost being killed for that smile alone.

I smiled back, suddenly nervous. The music started; a soft version of the traditional bridal music played with stringed instruments. Dad and I began our slow walk past family and friends. I held Bloodbane in one hand, still decorated with a small number of roses. It seemed right somehow.

As I neared the end, Dad coughed and embraced me tightly. I returned the hug. He didn't let go. Mum stood and gently pulled him away and into a seat next to her in the front row. I mouthed a silent "thank you" and took my place next to Lorandir. My bridesmaids adjusted my dress as best they could and then stepped back.

Ironfist stood in front of us and Morthimas moved from Lorandir's side to join him. In turn, they welcomed everyone in their native languages before switching to English. Ironfist took the lead.

"Dearly beloved, we are gathered here today to witness the joining of Lorandir of the Evergreen palace and Amethyst Haernson. There is a saying that love conquers all and it is clear to me that I am in the presence of great love today. These two courageous souls have chosen love over hatred and prejudice and have risked all to be here today. They have elected to say their own vows and seal this pact with the exchanging of rings. Who has the rings?" Ironfist stared at Morthimas who shrugged and mimed patting down his tunic.

From the back of the hall, I heard Marco speak into his walkie talkie, "And go Errol."

My small pet wyrm sauntered down the aisle, his forked tongue flicking over his lips and smoke curling from his nostrils. Lorandir bent down and beckoned him over. The wyrm raced towards him and took the proffered piece of coal with relish. Lorandir's long fingers deftly untied the silk ribbon around Errol's neck and released two plain gold bands.

I allowed myself a small smile at the rings. I had created them myself and had used a technique that an elven smith had taught me to forge both mine and Lorandir's magical essence into the metal. Lorandir handed the larger of the rings to me and then met my eyes and began to recite his vows.

"Galad 'Amethyst, light of my life, today I take you to be my wife. The day we met was a fateful one. Since then, I have been a better, more complete person when I am at your side. I vow to love you, to treasure you and to be with you through sorrows and joys and to love you for always, for all the days of our life together."

As Lorandir slipped the ring onto my finger, I felt the familiar heat, honey mead and forest sensations of his magic mix with the warmth of firelight and sparking metallic flavour of my own power. It was a heady, intimate feeling.

My voice came out in a breathless whisper as I spoke my vow, "Lorandir, today I take you as my husband. It hasn't been an easy journey, but I choose to love you in the good times and the bad and cherish you for always, with a love as hard and as bright as the jewels that blaze in the earth." I watched Lorandir's face as I placed the ring on his finger and saw his surprise and then slow smile as he felt our merged magics in the metal band.

"And now, we sign the contract of marriage," Ironfist interrupted our shared moment. He gestured to a seated dwarf who quickly unfurled a fold-out table and unravelled two copies of scrolls laden with Dwarfish runes. An English translation had been copied out for Lorandir's benefit. Morthimas looked on amused and handed us two sturdy leaves on which our names had been written in flowing cursive underneath Lorandir's family crest of an oak tree growing from a single acorn. Elves did things very differently.

We signed each of the documents with a special pen that Ironfist presented us with while Maxi took endless photos of us sealing the marriage. Ironfist checked everything over carefully before heating a pool of red wax and pressing the heavy seal of the Dwarven High Council into it. He took one of the scrolls and passed it to his assistant for filing with the records of marriage in the archives of Jarnstradr. The other he handed to me. I had nowhere to keep it, so I passed it to Aloora, who tried, and failed, to fit it into her clutch bag. Mum stood and gestured for me to give it to her, and she squirrelled it away in the depths of her oversized satin handbag. Lorandir and Morthimas simply tucked the elven leaves into pockets sewn inside their embroidered tunics and shared a knowing smile about the elaborateness of dwarf contracts.

"And now, by the power vested in me by the Dwarven High Council…"

"And the power vested in me as King of the Elves," Morthimas interjected. They continued together as if they had rehearsed, "It is my, our, honour and great pleasure to declare you married. Go forth and live each day to the fullest. And now, you may seal this declaration with a kiss."

"Go on, kiss her!" Morthimas urged.

Lorandir smoothed back my hair, which had fallen in front of my face before bending down and claiming my mouth with his.

Cheers erupted from our guests, and we broke apart. I couldn't keep the smile off my face as we walked back down the aisle as husband and wife. I waved at everyone I knew. Dad blinked back tears. Uncle Owain and Dylan blubbed freely. Even Gran looked like she might be happy for us. Agent Jones gave me a small smile and a nod as we passed her while Dot grinned from ear to ear, exposing her fangs as she shared a thumbs up. Maxi crouched at the end of the aisle trying to get an artistic photo shot. We stepped over him into the cold late afternoon air for canapes and drinks.

Chapter 39

Marco muttered into his walkie talkie again and servers in red waistcoats appeared from inside the castle. They served mulled white wine and tiny Welsh cakes on silver platters. I helped myself to a glass of the warm drink and fished out the tiny orange fruit floating in it before taking a long drink.

Lorandir handed me a Welsh cake before I even asked. The elf knew me so well. I chewed the sweet cake, savouring the taste. It seemed like a long time since I'd last eaten.

Maxi bustled over and ushered us into a group shot in front of the rebuilt castle. The pictures ended with a confetti shot that Maxi insisted on redoing three times to get the perfect blend of me and Lorandir kissing, the guests smiling and the delicate dried rose petals suspended in the air. In the end, one of the elves let out a small burst of magic to keep the confetti hanging in mid-air so he could get his shot.

While our guests carried on enjoying the canapes, Maxi whisked Lorandir and I away for what he called 'couple's shots'. Marco hovered by his side, clipboard in hand, as he checked through our schedule.

As the light faded further, Marco led us back towards the castle. Cheerful warm lights lit the windows from within. Maxi flew his drone around us, taking more pictures as we walked. I tried not to snap at him, but my cheeks ached from smiling so much for the dzraking photos.

Inside, the vaulted cellar room had been transformed with round tables set out neatly. I noted the burgundy bows tied around the chairs and silently thanked Marco for his tasteful choice in decorations. The elves had restrained themselves to small round vases filled with more red and white roses, trimmed with arches of delicate green reeds in intricate twists. Everyone stood as we entered and gave another cheer. I raised our clasped hands up above my head in acknowledgement and we headed to the top table.

As we passed Gunther and Bethan, I noted the shiny crystal shapes on his waistcoat embroidered with glowing purple thread. He gave me a wave and a wink as I stared at the loud waistcoat. Bethan gave me a wink too as she pressed his back, and the crystals began to flash on and off. With something approaching horror, I realised there were LEDs embedded into the waistcoat. I tore my gaze away and focused on getting to my seat.

Mum was sitting between Morthimas and Lorandir's Dad. She seemed happy enough and Bovolmiras smiled between sips of drink. Aloora was on his other side and chatting away in fluent Elvish about something. Lorandir's Mum looked down her straight nose at my Dad and ignored Espretha two seats away. She brightened up a little when Marco took the empty seat next to her but otherwise seemed quiet. I slipped into my seat next to Dad and Lorandir took his place at my side. Lorandir's Mum reached for the wine and the trailing sleeve of her green dress brushed against a tea light candle on the table. Her dress caught alight, and she flapped her arm uselessly in an attempt to put it out.

The waving motion only fanned the flames and she screamed. Dad jumped up and threw a jug of water over her. The flames were doused instantly, and the regal elf managed a smile of thanks at the dwarf by her side.

The food arrived quickly. One of the benefits of being the ones getting married is that you're served before anyone else, so as soon as our starters of mini sausage sandwiches arrived, complete with brown sauce and ketchup, I tucked into Brinda's excellent cooking straight away. She came out after the main course – a classic roast - had been served to check everything had been alright.

"It was amazing as always Brinda, thank you so much," I gushed.

She blushed prettily in her dark blue sari, trimmed with gold thread and told me it was nothing. Then she turned to Marco. It was clear who was running this wedding. He gave the nod, and she left the room before returning with a trolley bearing a cake almost as tall as I was. It was beautiful. There were six tiers covered with white icing. Gold stars, which I later learned were moulded chocolate, decorated the sides and the topper was a large dragon sculpture made of icing.

I stood and rushed over to study it more closely. Its wings swept up towards the ceiling as if it were landing. Gold dust picked out the details of its scales over the deeper red under colour.

"Thank you, Brinda, it's…wonderful," impulsively, I pulled her into a hug and she rewarded me with a large smile before standing back with her camera phone at the ready.

"And now a picture of you two cutting the cake please."

I looked around for a kitchen knife. Brinda's eyes widened as she realised she'd forgotten it. Before she could rush back into the kitchen, Espretha appeared by Lorandir's side. She flicked her wrist and a long silver dagger materialised in her palm. She handed it to me with a wink. Carefully, we cut the cake.

I almost moaned as I recognised the dark chocolate brownie that made up the top tier. That was definitely for me. Lorandir took his hands off the axe and broke off a small piece. He fed it to me. I sucked his fingers as I took the rich brownie and buttercream from his hand and his eyes heated with lust. A flash reminded us that we were still on display and Maxi was determined to chronicle every intimate moment.

With a knowing smile, Brinda took the trolley out and reappeared almost instantly with platters laden with different kinds of iced cakes which she offered around. I took a piece of the brownie cake, obviously, and another slice of red velvet cake. Dzrak it was delicious.

Marco stood and tapped his spoon on the edge of his glass, creating a tinging noise that carried over the noises of enjoyment from the guests. They quietened down and Marco announced that it was time for speeches.

Dad stood and fumbled with a piece of paper. He squinted at it and held it at arm's length before Mum handed him his reading glasses. Once they were on, he started his speech in a booming voice, "I never thought I'd see the day when a daughter of mine would be married to an elf. I mean, it's not like they're our natural allies," a hush fell over the room as he paused as if he'd told a joke.

I felt my face redden and I squeezed Lorandir's hand in silent apology under the table, "but it appears that she has taken after me when it comes to love and followed her own path." Here, he shared a loving look with Mum that had me blushing even more, "Ahem, anyway, as I was saying, our Amethyst has always been different. I remember when she was a youngling, she insisted on a hammer and tongs for toys instead of dolls or building blocks…" Dad's eyes misted over as he got lost in the memory of me as a child.

Mum coughed and nudged him, "Er, yes, where was I? Well here she is today and I know she has once again chosen her own path. Amethyst, I wish you and Lorandir every happiness together and Lorandir, welcome to the family, son." Dad raised his glass and took a long drink before he stepped around me and pulled my shocked husband into a bear hug. Tears flowed openly down Dad's face now, and he sniffed before giving me a hug too. He moved back to his seat and Mum handed him a handkerchief from her bag.

Lorandir stood next. He appeared his usual confident self, but I caught the tremble of his hands that betrayed his nerves. "First, I want to say how beautiful my lovely bride looks," he raised his glass to me and everyone else followed suit. I smiled weakly and tried to remember how I had looked this morning before the fight. "And I also want to thank her. I have been alive for a century and my life was meaningless before she blazed into it. I only hope I can bring her a modicum of the happiness she has brought me," he turned his gaze on me and I beamed back at him.

"To the lovely Amethyst." He raised his glass and toasted me before starting to sit. Then he seemed to remember something, and he stood again, "And thank you for being here with us today," He raised his glass again to a murmur of laughter as the guests realised they were definitely an afterthought.

Morthimas stood gracefully and smiled at the room, "Well cousin, as King I want to say that I think you ably demonstrated why you are not the best diplomat for the elves," this time the laughter was louder, "but as best man, I understand it is my job to tell embarrassing stories about the groom…my problem was narrowing it down!" More laughter erupted, particularly from the elven guests. Even Lorandir's Mum's lips were twitching into a smile.

"Elves are blessed with long life spans, which means there are plenty of opportunities for embarrassment. I could tell you about the time he ended up naked in front of the elven court, or more recently his attempts to outdrink a dwarf on his stag do…" Cheers broke out from my dwarven family at this. I looked at Lorandir questioningly as his ears turned pink; there was definitely a story here.

"But instead, I decided to speak of love. I have known Lorandir for over a century and I have never known him to be as happy or alive as he is with Amethyst. She is the best thing to happen to him and I am truly glad they found each other. It is a testament to love that it can cross any barrier and a testament to their courage that they have chosen to be together and share that love. To Amethyst and Lorandir."

The elf raised his glass and toasted us before speaking again, "And to love! May we all be so blessed to find it!" After raising his glass again, Marco caught his eye and Morthimas clapped his hands together, "And now I understand it is time to dance, please head through the door to the dancefloor."

Marco waited for us all to walk up the small flight of steps into the dancefloor. I inhaled sharply as we entered. The room took my breath away. The wooden floors were polished to a high shine that reflected the light from ornate chandeliers. Facsimiles of medieval paintings surrounded by Latin text decorated the walls.

A white castle trimmed with gold served as a mantelpiece over the large fireplace. Arches lined the room in different styles that ranged from Moorish to simple medieval style were trimmed with gold leaf. It was overwhelming.

Then Marco announced our first dance, and I noticed Maxi dart to a speaker set in the corner. He flipped a switch before whipping out his camera. Elvis Presley's crooning voice filled the space. Lorandir took my hand and pulled me into the centre of the room. As we started to sway to *Fools Rush In*, I focused on his bright green eyes and the start of the rest of our life together.

Epilogue

The rest of the night passed in a blur. I remember Dad blubbing as we danced together and the look in Lorandir's Mum's eyes when I paired her up with Dad for a dance. She'd hissed something to her son, but he'd shrugged and replied in English that it was tradition.

His Dad seemed to be having fun dancing with my Mum anyway and he twirled her gracefully before calling to his wife to join in. I smiled mischievously and grabbed another drink. All my hens grabbed me for a boogie to our self-proclaimed anthem *Girls just wanna have fun*. Gary the gargoyle insisted on a dance too. He was slow on his feet and when his hands drifted towards my butt, I swatted him away.

"If 'oo ever get tired of the elf, give me a call, sweet cheeks," he leered.

"Oh, dzrak off Gary before I get Mim to curse you again."

He laughed, a gravelly sound before moving off to try to accost some of the other female guests. A table appeared around ten o'clock, laden with bacon baps. I tried to find Brinda to thank her, but she'd gone so instead I ate two of the delicious sandwiches and enjoyed the crispy, salty flavour while I watched the dancing.

I caught Aloora slow dancing with the red-headed Shesalva. I'd insisted that we invite the elven librarian and was glad to see my match making had paid off. I gave my friend a wave and she winked at me before closing her eyes and snuggling closer with the tall elf.

Towards the end of the night, I gathered up my axe from the corner where I'd left it when Ironfist cornered me. He had a drink in hand and a scroll in the other. I stared at the small dwarf as he balanced both objects and dug in his pockets for something. He produced a small bag with flourish and handed it to me. I opened the black velvet bag first and tipped it carefully. A heart-shaped carnelian stone fell into my hand.

"It's a small gift for you, to encourage…"

"Thank you," I cut him off. I knew what the stone's properties were; it encouraged desire and fertility. I had no desire to discuss my sex life with a member of the Dwarven Arms Council. He gave me a knowing look.

"And one more thing," he lifted a finger and handed me the scroll, "Another of your ancestors used Bane, which we now know is Bloodbane, to fight alongside the elves. There were rumours at the time of a romance with an elven princess," he looked meaningfully from me to Lorandir, who was laughing at something Espretha had said. I blushed. "This is the only copy of a poem written about them. It's been hidden in our archives because, well, it's quite erotic and it flatters an elf, which is something us dwarves have not been able to stomach.

You see, history repeats itself…it's fate that you two are together."

The Councilmember turned and bustled off to join Morthimas and Lorandir's parents, ever the diplomat. I stared after him and opened the scroll tentatively. My face heated.

Not only was it a dirty poem, it was illustrated too. I tilted my head at one of the drawings in confusion. How the dzrak did they manage that? I hastily rolled up the scroll and retrieved Bloodbane from the corner of the room before heading to Lorandir's side.

We had just stepped outside with the cheers of our drunken guests reeling behind us when an explosion sounded. I gripped Bloodbane tightly, ready to fight. Lorandir pointed up.

Fireworks lit up the dark winter's sky. I turned and met Maxi and Madam Mim's bright smiles. I mouthed thank you at them, then turned to look at my elf. I stood on my tiptoes and kissed him.

Dzrak fate. We had chosen to be together, and we would have our happily ever after.

Bonus Chapter – Lorandir's Stag Do

Lorandir gingerly felt the reindeer antlers that his friends had placed on his head. He wasn't sure this was part of the stag do customs, but Morthimas had insisted so now he was wearing the dzraking things and looking like a fool. He looked around the restaurant, "Explain to me again how this is a 'send-off'?"

"Well, it's your stag do, you know, the last big night of freedom, yah? Your last chance for full on debauchery and meaningless sex before you get shackled by marriage."

Lorandir nibbled some chicken as he considered Maxi's reply. Their table was getting plenty of inviting looks from the female staff thanks to the innate elven glamour that surrounded him, his cousin the King and the Morty's single bodyguard.

"And Amethyst would be alright with this?" his brows furrowed in confusion as he pictured the petite fiery dwarf, hands on hips, nostrils flaring and brown eyes narrowed if he was ever stupid enough to ruin their bond by sleeping with someone else. No, his fiancée would not be happy.

Maxi looked around the group for support as he struggled for an answer, "Er..."

"It's tradition!" Gunther came to his aid and clapped the tall elf on the shoulder, "Besides, the real tradition is good food, good drink and male bonding." The confident dwarf ordered another pitcher of beer.

"And you are the only one of us about to be shackled, cousin, the rest of us can debauch if we want to..." Morthimas, King of the elves, smiled encouragingly at the tall human who bent to place the jug of beer on the table. He turned in his seat to watch her sashay away and smiled again as she sent him a saucy look over her shoulder before flicking her long hair. He was relishing in the small freedom from his new kingly duties. His guard frowned and moved uncomfortably in his seat, evidently not enjoying his king's enjoyment.

Lorandir finished his fried chicken, "So what exactly does male bonding on a stag do look like?"

"I looked it up on the internet. Apparently in Britain, it is drinking, food and making fools of yourselves..."

"And strip clubs!" Maxi interrupted Marco's explanation.

"We will not be visiting a strip club. I checked. That is optional."

Lorandir sided with Marco, "This is to celebrate my commitment to Amethyst, why would I want to go to a strip club?"

"Exactly, why get milk out when you've got cream at home!" Gunther smiled, but the rest of the group looked puzzled.

"I don't think that translated well, but no strip clubs," Lorandir said firmly.

Maxi looked put out but soon perked up, "But we will be going to bars yah? I remember when Bertie, my friend from school got married, it was a disaster! We got so drunk he chundered everywhere. Poor chap! They found him next morning naked in the street tied to a lamppost with no eyebrows!" He laughed to himself at the memory, "Anyway, bottoms up!" He downed his glass of beer and wiped his mouth with the back of his hand, "Where to next?"

Lorandir grimaced as he drank down his own beer. He preferred the sweeter taste of mead or elven wine but apparently on stag dos, one drank tepid beer. Marco checked his phone. He'd planned the whole evening with Aloora to make sure the couple didn't meet up. He nodded, his dark hair flopping over his eyes and looked up.

"Next, we go to a bar!"

Gunther helped Maxi finish up the pitcher of beer and the stags headed out into the cold night air. It was a short walk to the bar. Lorandir glanced at the sign swinging in the stiff breeze. A pentagram surrounding a drop of red blood. As they entered, the sickly-sweet smell of spilled spirits assaulted the elf's keen senses. He wrinkled his nose as he acclimatised himself. Another aroma lurked beneath the fruity overtones of alcohol. It smelled metallic and meaty. His eyes opened wide as he recognised the scent of blood.

"What is this place?"

A hostess appeared in front of them, "Welcome to Blud, do you have a reservation?" Marco flashed his phone at the attractive lady in a smart waistcoat over a crisp white shirt. "Very good sir, if you'll please follow me."

She led them to a booth and handed out cocktail menus, "I'm Laetitia and I'll be your server this evening. I'll let you peruse our drinks and will return momentarily to take your order. If you need anything, please don't hesitate to call me." She turned to go but paused as Gunther laid his hand on her wrist.

"What do you recommend fair Laetitia?"

She gave a smile that showed her fangs and pointedly looked at the dwarf's hand. He removed it, but kept the grin on his face. "Our most popular drink is the Bloody Bellini."

"Excellent! A round of those please, and something special for the stag."

The vampire took in the set of antlers on Lorandir's head and gave him a sympathetic smile before heading to the bar. In less than a minute she was back with a tray of red drinks in tall champagne flutes with sugar vampire fangs balancing on the edge of the glasses. She handed them out and then pushed a shot glass in front of Lorandir. She gave him a wink before walking away.

"Cheers to the stag!" The group raised their glasses before drinking the cocktails. They were sweet and fruity. Much better than the beer, Lorandir thought. Morthimas ordered his frowning guard to have one too. The guard furrowed his brows trying to decide if he should disobey an order from his King.

"Come on elf! Have a drink!"

The rest of the stags caught on and chanted "Drink!" until the poor guard downed the fruity cocktail. Morthimas gave a sly smile and ordered another round.

"So, cousin, tell us how you knew Amethyst was the one."

Lorandir considered as he sipped his drink, "I think it was when she drew her axe on me for the first time…"

"That sounds like our Ame!" Gunther guffawed as he slapped the elf on the back.

"She was the only woman who didn't throw herself at my feet. She seemed impervious to elven glamour and more than that, she challenged me. I feel like a bumbling idiot around her when all I want to do is impress her. I would risk everything to protect her and love her."

Morthimas paused in his admiration of a nearby group of women and screwed up his elegant face as he tried to understand, "So her not being enthralled by you is what made you love her?" It was a completely alien concept for the glamourous elf to grasp. He glanced at his bodyguard and pushed another Bellini his way before returning the smile of a curvy blonde.

"It is more than that," Lorandir sighed as he tried to put into words his feelings for the half-dwarf, "In my century on this earth, I have never felt more alive than when I am with her. She burns with a fire I have never experienced, and I want to be burned. She is the mate of my soul; I am sure of it and I am humbled she has chosen me out of all other males. I wish you could experience true love too."

"It sounds magical," Marco replied wistfully. The other stags were quiet. They all took a long drink as they contemplated their own romantic experiences.

"Enough of this maudlin talk you lot. Time for another stag do tradition – drinking games!" Gunther announced as he called for a round of Blud's finest shots, coupled with beer chasers and a yard of mead for the stag.

Lorandir swayed into his bathroom and threw up noisily. He hadn't ever been this drunk before and it was awful. He shouldn't have agreed to the shots. He especially shouldn't have let them tell him that he had to drink two because he was the stag. And he definitely shouldn't have been comforted when Gunther had said he would drink the same amount. Bloody dwarves. He threw up again. A sheen of sweat appeared on his golden skin. The door opened behind him and Amethyst burst into the small room. She gave him a look that was part amusement, part concern and helped him to the sofa. He wanted to speak, to tell her she was his everything, but the small woman disappeared from view. When she returned, she shoved a glass of water into the elf's long hands and commanded him to drink. He nodded and downed the water before blinking up at her. She had a garish pink sash over her body that made his eyes hurt. He focused on the plastic tiara in her hair and raised one hand up to tug it free. Dzrak, he loved it when her wild hair was free and falling around her face.

"You look like a princess," he smiled then closed his eyes and fell back against the sofa, snoring softly.

Thank you

A massive thank you as ever to my awesome husband who is not only supportive but is also the first person to read any of my stories.

And a huge thank you to my patreon supporter: Emma Ward, who always believes in me.

A special thanks to Kat, who gave me permission to parody the time she got bitten by a squirrel – it was the inspiration for the pictsie bite!

To my terrific typo hunters and brilliant beta readers, you made this story better than it started.

And to you, wonderful reader, thank you for picking up this book and even reading the thank you page – you are amazing!

If you enjoyed this book, you can get a free prequel to my Rise of Dragons series by signing up to my mailing list on www.gemmaclatworthy.com. And join the conversation at Gemma's book wyrms or see all my books before they're published on patreon.com /G_Clatworthy.

As an independent author, your reviews help me decide which series to keep going so please do leave one for Fated Bloodlines, and if you enjoyed this book, check out the Omensford series, set in the same universe.

About the Author

Gemma started writing during the 2020 lockdown and loves fantasy fiction and dragons in particular. She lives in Wiltshire with her family and two cats and also enjoys crafts of all kinds. You can see all her writing on patreon.com/G_Clatworthy. Join the conversation at Gemma's book wyrms readers' group on Facebook.

She also writes children's books. You can find out more on her website www.gemmaclatworthy.com or follow her on Instagram (www.instagram.com/gemmaclatworthy) or Facebook (www.facebook.com/gemmaclatworthy).

Other Books by G Clatworthy

Books in the Rise of the Dragons series:

<u>Awakening</u>

<u>Solstice of Dragons</u>

<u>Equinox Betrayal</u>

<u>Darkest Deception</u>

<u>Attack on Avalon</u>

<u>Fated Bloodlines</u>

Books in the Omensford series (set in the Rise of Dragons universe) [Coming soon]:

Bedsocks and Broomsticks

Cream Teas and Crystal Balls

Demons and Donkeys

Children's Books

The Child Who series:

The Girl Who Lost Her Listening Ears
The Boy Who Lost His Listening Ears
The Girl Who Dreamed of Sleep
The Boy Who Dreamed of Sleep

Other books:

Coronavirus in the words of children